I0763590

Touched

Speculative and Flash Fiction

Russ Towne

Touched: Speculative and Flash Fiction
Published by Russ Towne.

Second Edition

www.RussTowne.com
RussTowne@yahoo.com

ISBN 978-0-692-70008-2

Book Design by Gail Nelson, e-book-design.com

Printed in the United States

Dedication

This book is dedicated to all who bring my creations to life by reading them.

Contributors

Editor: Sandy Lardinois, JeWeL Publishing LLC

Proofreader: Shayla Eaton, curiousercditing.com (for material added since this title's first release)

Cover designer: Joleene Naylor

Book designer: Gail Nelson, e-book-design.com

Contents

Touched . . . 1
Afterglow . . . 11
No Choice at All . . . 17
Heartsight . . . 23
The "Misunderstanding" . . . 27
Here . . . 37
Desperation . . . 45
The Best Policy . . . 48
Hoodwinked . . . 50
Everyone Wins . . . 51
The Elm Street Ladies' Club . . . 53
Fool's Gold . . . 55
The Patsy . . . 58
For as Long as the Music Plays . . . 60
The Decision . . . 61
Helping the War Effort . . . 63
Hope . . . 64
The Mob . . . 68

The Despicable Coward 70
OOPS! 71
Epiphany. 72
It Had Been So Easy 75
Suicide Mission 78
Without a Hitch 81
Hard Bargain 83
Crescendo 84
Inseparable 86
Saddle Buddies 87
The Fog. 88
Fog of War 89
A Fairy Tale for Grown-up Children. 90
Piggyback 93
Irony 95
Coming Out Party 96
Interstellar Invitation 97
Bonus Material 104
I Only Wanted to Be Their Friend 105
Tough Night at the Lumber Mill 108
Terror on Interstate 5 113
Blood Oaths 121
Legacy. 137
Nightmare. 146
About the Author 155

Touched

Tom came out of curiosity and a sense of adventure. He knew almost nothing about the woman he stood in line for an hour to meet. It was clear Baaza was from another country and culture, and she appeared to speak little English. She wore a colorful outfit and sat cross-legged on bright pillows in the center of the stage, briefly greeting each person in a long line of folks waiting to meet her.

Baaza was known as the "Toucher of Hearts." Tom understood why when he felt all the love filling the huge room. The energy felt unlike anything he'd experienced in such a large crowd. Love. Pure love. It felt good, as though he were being bathed in it. He wondered whether those with so much love in their hearts were attracted to Baaza or whether she was the reason they had so much love in their hearts.

When it was Tom's turn to meet Baaza, he knelt in front of her as he saw the others do. She looked into his eyes and placed both hands over his heart. In an instant, his body and spirit felt light, like huge burdens were lifted from them. The room began to spin. He noticed a look of shock and amazement on Baaza's face, and heard her exclaim, "You're the one!" Then he blacked out.

When he came to, the room was nearly dark and empty, except for Baaza, an interpreter, and him.

Touched

With the help of the interpreter, Baaza said, "I'm glad to see you are okay. I had a dream many years ago. In it, I touched a young man's heart, and the joining of our energies created a great gift within him. You are that man. I knew it the moment I touched your heart and felt the joining of our energies. Did you feel it too?"

"I felt something amazing when you touched me," Tom began. "I felt a great lightness; my worries and problems disappeared."

"That is good to hear because along with the great gift comes a terrible burden."

"What is the great gift?"

"You have the gift of healing."

"Like a doctor?" Tom asked.

"No, far more powerful and immediate than any doctor."

He laughed. "Surely you're joking! I'm no healer!"

"You might not have been one before, but you are now."

"Even if I believed you, and I'm not saying I do, what's the catch—that terrible burden you mentioned?" Tom's disbelief was becoming a growing concern.

"When you cure someone, it will require great energy and life force, so you'll sacrifice part of your life and health each time you do it."

"Oh." Tom thought for a moment. "I don't want the gift. I don't want to be faced with such choices. Whatever you did, please undo it!"

"I truly wish I could, but I can't, no more than you can. What's done is done. I'm sorry."

Dazed, Tom said good-bye and walked back to his car. He felt a light tap on his shoulder. It was the interpreter. "I'm sorry to ask this of you, but I'm desperate. My sister's baby is dying of an inoperable brain tumor and not expected to live much longer." She started sobbing. "Will you please help me? I know I'm asking a lot, and what it will cost you, and I have no right to ask, but—"

Tom cut her off. "I doubt I have the power to heal, but if it will make you feel better, I'll try."

A look of great relief swept over her face. "Thank you, thank you so much! Can we go to the hospital right now?"

"It's two a.m., and I'm exhausted."

"Emerald may not make it through the night. Won't you please come now?"

Over an hour later, Tom awkwardly held the dying baby while Emerald's parents and aunt looked on with hope and desperation etched on their faces. He didn't know what he was supposed to do and was terrified of disappointing them. Tom cradled Emerald in one arm and lightly touched her forehead with the fingers of his other hand. He felt like he was about to black out again and quickly handed the baby to her mother.

He came to in a hospital bed and found he'd slept for nearly twelve straight hours, yet still felt tired. His room was covered in thank-you notes, flowers, and balloons. He read the cards and couldn't believe it. Baby Emerald had made a full recovery and there was no trace there had ever been a tumor.

He smiled. It felt great emotionally to have helped Emerald and her family, but it physically *hurt* him. Every muscle and joint ached. He decided he'd had enough of this healing business and got dressed to go home. *I'm no hero. I just want to live a normal life, without all this pain. I'm going to let doctors do the healing.*

As he headed for the door of his room, he noticed the interpreter had just been stopped by security guards who must have been guarding his room. She said something to them and walked in beaming. "I came to check on you. I'm so glad you're okay. You gave us quite a scare. Thank you for healing Emerald."

Tom nodded, a bit embarrassed. “I didn’t really do anything but touch her. By the way, I never learned your name.”

“Oh, I’m sorry. I’m Bethany. Most people call me Beth.”

“Thank you for checking on me.” He nodded toward the door. “Are they here to keep me in or keep someone out?”

Beth laughed, but caught herself and cut it short. “To keep others out. Word spread that you can heal people and a lot of folks have been trying to talk to you. It’s a hospital, after all. There are a lot of very sick people and their relatives here. The hospital posted guards so you could rest and the staff wouldn’t be pestered.”

“I want to get out of here.”

“You’ll get mobbed at the front doors if you do. Someone leaked the story to the press, and I heard a crowd has waited for several hours in front of your apartment. Even your car in the parking lot here has a crowd around it.”

“This is a nightmare!” Tom swallowed and his stomach churned. He felt trapped.

“I feel responsible for getting you into this mess. I’d like to help you if I can.” She thought for a moment. “I’ll be right back.”

Five minutes later she came back with the uniforms and ID badges of two interns.

“Don’t ask how I got ’em, just put ’em on. The surgical face mask and stethoscope too. They’ll help us slip out a side door that a staffer disarmed for us.”

As they quickly got in their disguises, she said, “You can’t go to your apartment. I can take you to my place until things settle down.”

“Thank you, Beth.”

“Let’s go!”

They got to her place without incident, but his disappearance was now making news and keeping the story alive. "It's time to get out of this city. Maybe I'll fly to my parents' in Denver."

Someone knocked on the door. Beth answered it to find a man holding a child who appeared to be about eleven but was wasted away so badly she couldn't stand. Her mother stood beside them. "One of your neighbors saw the miracle worker come here. She works with me and knows about our Susan. Please, may we speak to him?

Beth stood in the doorway, unsure what to do. Tom walked up. "Please come in."

"Please sit down, folks. I'll help you, but first you've got to promise that you won't tell anyone how your daughter was cured or where I am. Will you do that for me?"

"Wait, Tom, remember what happened last time? You better sit down first."

A minute later, Susan was cured and Tom had blacked out. He stayed unconscious for fourteen hours this time, but he felt even worse than he did with Emerald. Weaker. Older.

At 2:30 a.m., a pounding on their door woke them up. *Someone must have crawled over the back fence,* Tom thought as he rose from the couch and went to the door to see who it was. A gun was jammed in his face by someone who looked to be in his late teens. He'd been shot in the shoulder and had lost so much blood that he fainted a moment later. Tom took the gun, healed the gunman, and blacked out.

When Tom awakened late that morning, Beth said, "He's gone, but he told me what happened. His name is Dwight. His dad's in prison. His mom borrowed money from loan sharks and they'd been leaning real hard on her. He bought a gun to try to scare them off, but they pulled out their own guns. Dwight got scared, shot one in the leg, and ran. They shot him from behind. He knew better than go to a hospital with a gunshot wound right after there'd been a shooting so he came here. He saw how much it damaged you to help him, and he asked me to thank you for him. He said he hoped he could do something for you someday."

Beth's phone rang. Word got out about where Tom was and the lives he saved. They disconnected the phone after the sixth caller in ten minutes. A steady stream of people knocked on her door. A small crowd gathered.

"One of the people who came to the door while you were unconscious offered you twenty thousand dollars to heal his mother. I think it was every penny he had."

Tom rested his head in his hand. "I don't know what to do. I can't help everybody, and I don't know how long my body will be able to stand the strain. It's like the more I help people, the more I get punished for doing it." He looked at Beth. "And now I've dragged you into this mess. I'm so sorry."

Beth sat next to him and gave him a big hug. Their eyes met and lingered. They smiled and hugged again.

"Thank you, I needed that," he whispered.

"We're in this together and we'll deal with it together," Beth said with conviction. She went to the window. "Crowd's growing. I'm calling the cops."

Soon the police had dispersed the crowd, or, at least, broken them into smaller groups a bit farther away. Another knock on the door. Beth looked through the peephole and was relieved to see it was a police officer. She opened it. "Please come in."

The cop looked down at his feet and appeared to be building up his courage to say something. "I could get fired for asking you this, but our son, Johnny, nearly drowned eight years ago when he was seven, and his brain was so badly damaged that doctors say he'll never mentally mature beyond the age of a seven-year-old." Tears filled his eyes as he fought to maintain control. "It's killing me to see him like that. Please, I beg you, please help him. I don't have much money, but you can have all my savings if you'll help him."

Tom read his nametag. "That won't be necessary, Officer White. Bring him here, and I'll do what I can."

Officer Stan White was so relieved by his son's immediate transformation and so concerned at what happened to Tom when he healed Johnny, that he blurted to Beth, "I have a month's leave coming. You're essentially trapped in here. My family and I would like to offer our services to you. I have three sons. Johnny is the youngest. I'm sure some of my buddies on the force will be happy to help too. We can help keep watch on you, and my wife and her friends can bring meals for all of us."

"That's a wonderful offer, but we can't pay any of you."

"Tom and you already have. Please let us pay you both back in some small measure for saving my son."

By the time Tom woke up, everything was in place. Some of Beth's friends also pitched in. Tom was new to the area, but his two closest friends jumped on the first available plane when he called. They were shocked to see their friend. He looked twenty years older than when they'd seen him five months before. His hair had thinned and was more than half gray.

Tom decided that since he couldn't help everyone, he would focus only on babies, children, and pregnant mothers when their babies were at risk. In that way, the most life and years could be gained in exchange for the time and life he lost with each healing. The team set up a system of triage where he'd heal the one who was closest to death that day.

Sadly, some didn't live long enough for him to save them. It broke his heart with every loss, but he knew if he didn't pace himself, he'd save fewer children before he died.

Tom's joints ached all the time now. He tried several times to cure himself, but it never worked.

Tom and Beth grew to love each other, and the feeling grew stronger every day.

"Let's get married," Beth said one afternoon.

"There is nothing more I'd like to do if I was healthy, but I'm not, and you'd soon be married to a corpse."

"I'll treasure whatever time we have left together, as I've treasured all the time we've had until now. *Please.*"

They were married at her place on a hot day in July. The wedding made headlines around the world.

A week later, Beth said, "Baaza's coming back to town. Maybe we can meet with her."

Tom smiled weakly. "If I last that long."

Beth begged him to stop healing people, at least for a while.

"I can't. Too many people are counting on me. Too many lives at stake."

Beth arranged for a meeting with Baaza to occur on a Saturday afternoon. By then, Tom was so weak that Stan White and one of his friends wrapped one of Tom's arms over each of their shoulders and half-dragged, half-carried him to the door.

They'd arranged a full police escort. On the way, just before the car carrying Tom and Beth got to an intersection, a drunk sped through a red light and slammed into a small car carrying a young mother, an infant, and toddler. The police vehicles stopped, called for ambulances, and began to administer first aid. Tom opened a window and heard a senior officer say over the radio, "Their car is crushed. I don't think any of them will survive."

Tom yelled, "Bring me to them." He was carried over to the young mother and her children as they were extricated by the Jaws of Life. "If I black out after the first one, please touch my hand to the foreheads of the other two."

"No! That could kill you," Beth screamed, and began sobbing.

Tom came to in Baaza's arms. She smiled at him and touched his heart with both her hands. His body and spirit felt light, just like the first time. But something felt different. It took him a moment to realize his joints no longer ached. In fact, he felt fine, young, healthy, and alive! Beth held his hand. She was crying, but they were tears of joy.

As Beth translated, Baaza said, "I had another dream. Remember that young man you saved named Dwight who'd been shot? I saw him in my dream, tracked him down, and scheduled a meeting with him for when I came back into town. We met an hour ago. I told him everything. He asked me to touch his heart. When I did, our energies mixed, and he now has the gift and the burden that you carried so well. He touched you while you were blacked out and you became as young and healthy as when you and I first met. When you were cured, you lost the gift and the burden; he now carries both."

"But... but, the same thing will happen to him that happened to me." Tom looked around and saw Dwight blacked out on a couch.

"He knew that, Tom. He said he owed it to you for giving up so much when you saved him. He was grateful to be able to do the same for you."

Tom felt immense gratitude and relief.

Baaza paused. "Who knows? Maybe I'll have another dream in time to save him."

Beth added, "I hope so. I feel sad for him."

"I want to be here when he wakes up," Tom said through a huge yawn.

"We've got a bed made up for you and Beth." She pointed to a room down a hall. "Get some sleep. I'll let you know when he wakes up."

"Thank you," Tom and Beth said in unison. They held hands as they walked toward the bed and a new life together.

Afterglow

I could tell as we drove up that it was love at first sight. My wife Jennifer couldn't take her eyes off the secluded old house. The real estate agent, seeing her reaction and knowing a sale was almost certain, nearly leapt from the car. Martha looked to be around fifty-five years old, about twenty years our senior. She guided us from the front of the house to a small wall, which stood as a lonely sentinel protecting the unsuspecting from an eighty-foot drop to a rugged boulder-strewn beach. The surf mercilessly pounded unyielding, jagged rocks, but the latter gave no quarter, breaking up the attack and forcing the mighty waves to eventually retreat and regroup to strike yet again. I never tire of watching such epic battles, and was delighted to know that we could soon have daily ringside seats to this awesome spectacle. I was nearly as excited as Jennifer.

Martha turned and led us toward the large Victorian Era home. It reminded me of a beautiful woman who sat anxiously watching and waiting for her sailor to return from the sea.

Despite all of its natural beauty and architectural elegance, I couldn't shake the feeling that the house somehow exuded a sadness and loneliness that I couldn't explain.

Martha guided us from room to room, describing attributes as she went. She wisely slowed down to let us take in the amazing craftsmanship and decorative flourishes that were everywhere. It was obvious the old house had been well taken care of for most of its long existence, but the last few years clearly had been less kind to her. It was as though an elegant lady a bit past her prime had just stopped caring for herself. Small signs of recent neglect were evident, but clearly correctable with the tender love we were eager to begin lavishing on her.

It wasn't long before we were sitting at a table back in Martha's office putting an offer together. She paused, shifted in her chair, and looked down on the paperwork as she began speaking. Martha stammered. It appeared she was forcing herself to say something so distasteful that each word might well have been covered in lemon juice. "Uh, like some other houses along the coast, this house has had, shall we say, a 'colorful' history. Due to its secluded location during Prohibition, it was used by rumrunners to offload and store the moonshine brought in by boats. It then became a speakeasy and, uh, a house of ill repute."

Martha watched nervously at our reaction to the news. We looked at each other and began laughing. Jennifer quipped, "Well, that will certainly make for some interesting conversation at cocktail parties!" We all burst out laughing, and Martha's relief was palpable.

Now that Martha knew it was a safe subject, she added with a mischievous grin: "Local legend has it that police officers and sheriff's deputies came from many miles around and were some of the house's best customers."

Martha suddenly became quiet again, a troubled look replacing her laughter. "There is something else I need to tell you. A woman died in her sleep in this house about a year ago."

My heart sank. Jennifer is terrified of ghosts and has never liked being in buildings where people had died. Once several years ago at a tiny old restaurant, we read on their menu that many people believed the place was haunted. It described in detail several frightening incidents that had occurred on the premises. Most of them happened in the women's restroom. We noticed that the dining area was dimly lit, and the long, narrow, nearly dark hallway to the restrooms appeared to only have a single lonely, dust-covered, old-style 40-watt incandescent lightbulb. It cast an eerie yellow glow over the part of the hallway it could reach. The women's restroom appeared to be just beyond the lit area.

As the meal progressed, Jennifer became more and more fidgety in her chair. When I finally asked her what was wrong, she whisper-blurted, "I *really* need to go to the bathroom, but I don't want to go anywhere near the women's restroom after reading the stories about the ghost."

We were at least twenty miles from the next restroom, and it was clear she wouldn't be able to hold out that long. I unsuccessfully tried to calm her down, and finally due to desperation on both our parts, she said she'd use the restroom if I stood just outside the door and promised to rush in if I heard her scream. I did as she asked, feeling more than a little silly standing so close to the women's restroom, and especially for the reason I was there. When she got inside, I think she broke speed records as she used the facilities and raced out. We've never been back to that restaurant.

Whenever I recall that incident, I normally wear a big grin and sometimes burst out laughing; but not the time we were in Martha's office. I just *knew* Jennifer wouldn't want to proceed with the offer, but it turned out her love for that house and the excitement about it being the home of her dreams overcame all other concerns, and we bought it.

Jenifer and I moved in several weeks later and nervously watched as storm clouds gathered on moving day. We'd had to move in the rain once before and didn't want a repeat of that miserable experience. Fortunately, the movers finished before the storm hit. As they left, a neighbor drove up in a dusty old pickup and introduced himself. George Hanson informed us that he and his wife Hilda lived on a farm about fifteen minutes away and were our nearest neighbors. Then, within the next five minutes, he proceeded to tell us every secret and foible he could think of about everyone who lived within a thirty-mile radius. I wasn't facing Jennifer, but I swear I heard her eyeballs rolling as she turned away in disgust at the nonstop dirt dump. I wondered when this horrific gossip had time to do any farming, and made a mental note to refrain from telling him anything I didn't want to have broadcasted to the world.

As I attempted to think of a polite excuse to send him on his way, he asked, "Did you hear about the young woman who died in your house?" We nodded. "Her name was Evelyn. She was sweet and died way too young. It's because of Johnny Gables and Madeline Johnson." He saw the puzzled looks on our faces and added, "The coroner said Evie—that's what my Hilda called her—died of a heart attack, but my Hilda believes she really died of a broken heart and loneliness. Evie was engaged to Johnny, but a week before the big wedding, she caught Johnny and her best friend Madeline Johnson in bed together. In one fell swoop, Evie lost her fiancé and best—actually, only—friend.

"Evie never recovered. She barely ate and rarely left the house. It was her safe haven. One of her relatives had built it way back in the late 1800s and it's always been in her family. Until now. Evie was the last of her line. Anyway, life just seemed to drain out of her.

"My Hilda often visited, bringing baked goods and checking on her. Then one day, Evie didn't answer the door. A sheriff's deputy found her dead in her bed. Appears she died in her sleep. Poor thing."

He then veered off onto another tangent, and it took twenty more minutes of suffering through more dirt-dishing before we could finally get him to leave. I think he was beginning to run out of ammunition anyway, and since it was clear he was going to get little more than a name, rank, and serial number from us despite his rude questions and probing, I guess he felt he needed to go elsewhere to begin to reload.

We breathed sighs of relief as he drove away. *Tap. Tap-tap.* I looked up just in time to get hit in the face by the start of a full-blown rainstorm. We shrugged and laughed as we ran into the house. The rain fell so hard and fast it felt and sounded as though we were under a small dam that had just burst. I looked nervously at the old ceiling and hoped the roof two floors above it was as water-tight as Martha had claimed.

We spent the rest of the afternoon and most of the evening hours getting to know our new home and figuring where to put things. The lights flickered and went out. Absolute darkness. I was in the middle of a maze of boxes in a strange house in darkness so complete I couldn't see an inch in front of me. Jennifer was in the kitchen two rooms away with many obstacles lying in the dark between us. I started to carefully make my way toward the direction I thought I remembered the kitchen was in. *Crash!*

Jennifer yelled, "You okay, honey?"

As I attempted to pick myself up, I leaned on a pile of what felt like boxes and knocked over another whole pile. Some of the items fell on top of me as I crashed back onto the floor. "Yes!" I yelled in a voice that sounded more perturbed than okay.

"Wait there. I think I know where... ah, here it is." She came walking toward me, trailing a sweet beam of light and burst out laughing at the mess I'd made. Fortunately, the boxes that fell onto me had been full of clothes and other light items.

It took forty minutes to find and light candles, but when we finished, we realized how romantic it was. Since it was also the first night in our new home, we celebrated with some bubbly, toasted to our new home, kissed, blew out the downstairs candles, and took the remaining lit ones up creaky stairs to our new bedroom. We flopped our box spring and mattress onto the floor and threw some blankets on them, then blew out the candles, crawled beneath the covers, and fell asleep as our heads hit our pillows.

I was awakened by a pulsing golden glow, like that from a large candle, but, when I opened my eyes, the light was gone. *What was that?* I looked at Jennifer, who'd always been a deep sleeper. True to form, she'd slept through whatever it was that had awakened me.

Her skin glowed. *Must be a reflection from the moon,* I thought, until I remembered the drapes and blinds were closed and the storm clouds had smothered the moon. I still looked to be sure. No light came in through the windows. My gaze fell back onto Jennifer. *What a beautiful woman I married,* I thought gratefully. My love for her was so deep I almost ached. At that moment, Jennifer opened her eyes and whispered, "Let's make love!" There was an urgency and hunger in her voice that I hadn't heard in years.

I knew from the moment we kissed that something was different. It was powerful and deep and lasted much longer than usual. We were both breathless when it ended.

Our love-making was more intensely passionate that night. We explored and pleasured each other's bodies as though for the first time, trying new things, rewarding and being rewarded.

When we were completely spent, Jennifer fell asleep almost instantly. I lay beside her in the dark, marveling at the magic we created, and was startled by a golden glow that rose from her sleeping body.

As it faded away, I heard the faintest whisper of a woman's voice I'd never heard before. "Thank you! It's been so long. Let's do it again sometime!"

No Choice at All

Daniel Hansen was angry, something he rarely felt for long. He got a flat tire on his way to the most important meeting of his career. It didn't help that it was a dark winter night. Daniel changed the tire, threw the flat in the trunk, and slammed the lid. The tire iron was still lying in the dirt where he'd left it. Daniel grabbed it and tossed it on the seat beside him before he sped away.

"Damn! So much for having extra time. I'll be okay if I don't have any more delays. Maybe have time to wash my hands."

Daniel increased his speed. His headlights tore into the darkness. The curves calmed him a bit as he got into a rhythm with the road. It had been perhaps twenty minutes since he'd seen a vehicle in the other lane.

He rounded a curve and sped toward two cars parked on the opposite side of the road. The dome light of the front car was on as he approached but went out as he was nearly abreast of it.

Daniel continued on his way. *"That's odd. The light went out, but the car's doors were open. Well, there could be good reasons for that."* But, as Daniel thought back to the scene, other things didn't seem quite right. A couple of men were on each side of the car and froze as he drove past.

"Was there a woman in the car? Yeah. With four men acting strange. On a dark road. In the middle of nowhere. Maybe it's just kids having fun. No.

Touched

The driver looked old enough to be their mother, and the men looked more like twenty-somethings than teens. Don't overreact. It may be nothing. Something innocent. Maybe they're helping her fix her car. And don't forget your interview. You stop now, and you can kiss the promotion and maybe even your job goodbye. What a choice!" Except, he knew it was no choice at all...

— —

Daniel Hansen's employer was a company founded by Harrison "The Dragon" Dunsmuir, who was a stickler for punctuality and many other things. Several people swore they actually saw fire spew from his mouth when he was angry. Daniel had seen a bit of Dunsmuir's temper, but, thankfully, it had always been directed at someone else. In every case, the young executive felt The Dragon was tough but fair.

Daniel began working for the company right out of college twelve years ago. He rapidly rose through the ranks and turned a poorly performing division into a well-oiled machine. While it was located far from headquarters, his successes came to the attention of Dunsmuir.

When the top executive of the division that was the crown jewel of the company announced his retirement, Daniel was asked if he was interested in being considered to replace him. Something like showing up late with dirty hands might not only ruin his chances for this job, it could put his future with the firm in jeopardy.

— —

Daniel found a place to turn around. *"How many curves has the road made since I saw the cars? Two? Three, and the last one was long and gradual. You better be right."* He drove past two curves and parked before the third. As he opened his door, he heard a woman scream. He tried to dial 911. *"No service!"*

Daniel saw the tire iron and grabbed it. He heard another scream. This time it was a man. Daniel raced to within a dozen feet of the car and stopped behind a tree. In the pale light of a half-moon, Daniel saw a man's fist smash into a young woman's jaw. She collapsed. A man grabbed her feet, another grabbed her by her slender wrists. She thrashed like a wounded lioness, freeing one of her legs. She kicked out wildly. Her foot connected with the kneecap of one of the men. He bellowed and grabbed his knee.

"Dammit, Jake! Hold her still," the wounded man yelled as they headed for the trees.

Daniel's eyes tried to focus through the blackness to the older woman. She was still behind the steering wheel but let go to punch the man standing in the open doorway to her left. He easily avoided her blows. The other man grabbed her hair and brutally yanked her onto the seat.

She was in more immediate trouble than the younger woman, but there was no way Daniel could take on men on both sides of the car without one raising the alarm and warning the other two.

He had to act. Now! The decision was made when the men reached the tree line with their prize.

Kneecap boasted, "Hellcat! The more you fight, the more fun we'll have, and the longer it's going to last." They dropped her, and Kneecap started ripping off her clothes as Jake held her down. She was fierce. But, they were bigger. Stronger. Heavier. And, there were two of them. Hellcat was losing the battle. It was only a matter of time.

Daniel crept up to them. With Jake's back toward him, Daniel swung the tire iron as hard as he could into his neck at the base of his skull. Kneecap was so focused on the struggling woman that it wasn't until he heard the sickening thud that he looked up to see Jake ragdoll to the ground. He inhaled to scream a warning to the others as Daniel sprang. Daniel swung the tire iron at Kneecap's neck to silence him, but Daniel tripped over one of the startled woman's thrashing arms. Instead of a crashing blow to the front of the neck, the tire iron swished through the air as Kneecap jerked backwards. Daniel crashed face first over the legs of the woman, and Kneecap pounced on him.

Hellcat's legs were pinned by the weight of the two struggling men, but her arms were free. She grabbed a handful of dirt and smashed it into Kneecap's face. Blinded, and with a mouth full of dirt, Kneecap could neither yell nor fight well. She clawed his face. He let go of his grip on Daniel's hand and leaned toward the woman.

Daniel pushed off the ground, twisted, and swung the tire iron up into Kneecap's head. He collapsed onto Hellcat and didn't move.

"Mom! She's in the car!"

Daniel pushed what was left of Kneecap off her and helped her up. They raced toward her mom. Hair-puller pinned her mother down by the shoulders. The other animal had pulled off his pants and was climbing into the car to mount her. Hellcat screamed and jumped onto Hair-puller's back. He spun out of the doorway and fell back onto her.

Pants-less' head jerked up as Daniel pulled him by his long hair completely over the woman and through the passenger-side doorway. He saw Hellcat doubled-over from a punch to the stomach. There was no time to fight Pants-less.

Daniel dropped him onto the ground, twisting his head sharply so the attacker ended up on his back. It was easy to decide where to hit him. Using both hands and his full bodyweight, he smashed the tire iron into the depraved monster's groin.

Daniel stood up, turned, and was thrown to the ground by Hair-puller. The tire iron flew out of Daniel's hand. The animal hit Daniel with a brutal shower of fists. Daniel tried to block the blows but was getting pummeled.

CRUNCH! Hair-puller crumpled. Hellcat had found the tire iron.

— —

They were exhausted, panting, and shaking. Daniel and Hellcat collapsed in heaps onto the ground. The older woman was still in the car. She moaned.

Daniel and Hellcat dragged themselves up and staggered over to where she lay, shivering. Hellcat said, "Sh-she's in shock." She pulled keys from the ignition. "S-suitcase." She shook her head, trying to shake the fog away. "Trunk. My clothes." She lifted the keys with a shaky hand to give them to Daniel, but they fell to the ground. She slumped against the car and slid to the dirt.

Daniel bent to pick up the keys and nearly fell over. *"We must all be in shock,"* he thought. He steadied himself with his arm sliding along the car as he walked to the trunk, opened it, and pulled out the suitcase. Daniel half carried, half dragged the suitcase to the ladies. He laid it down but shook so badly he couldn't open it the first two times. When it finally popped open, he laid out a couple of larger pieces of clothing in the dirt. Daniel helped Hellcat lie on them, then covered her with more clothes. He pulled out several more items, piled them on the floor of the car, and closed the suitcase lid. He elevated Hellcat's legs and pushed the suitcase under her calves to treat her shock symptoms; to allow more blood to return to her brain.

Daniel then went to help the older lady, but, as she saw him, she panicked, shrieked, and kicked him. Surprised, he fell backwards into the dirt. Brushing himself off, he crawled back, and tried again. "I won't hurt you. Please. Let me help. You're in shock."

The kicking continued, but only briefly. He didn't know whether it was because she believed him or because she was too exhausted to fight anymore. He was able to cover her. Daniel elevated her legs with a wad of clothes.

When he stood up, the world went black and he collapsed to the ground.

— —

Touched

Darkness. He heard voices. Women's voices. He started to open his eyes, but the world was spinning. He tried again. Slowly. His vision returned to normal. Hellcat and her mother were dressed. He tried to get up.

"Take it slow," Hellcat warned. "You were in shock. We all were."

"I should get you both to the hospital," Daniel said.

"No. We just want to go home. It's only a few miles away. Is your car nearby?"

Daniel nodded.

"We'll call the police from home."

Daniel nodded again.

"Mom was taking me to the airport when the car broke down, and those animals showed up. Thank you for stopping them."

"From what I saw, the two of you were putting up a hell of a fight before I came along."

"Fight or not, we were no match for them. We might not be alive if it weren't for you. Thank you. I'm Michelle, and this is my mom, Jean."

"Hi, I'm Daniel. Daniel Hansen."

The women looked at each other. That name. Jean said, "You wouldn't by any chance be on your way to meet Harrison Dunsmuir."

"H-How'd you know that?"

"Harrison's my husband."

— —

Daniel got the promotion.

A year later, Hellcat became his wife.

Daniel never did see his father-in-law, The Dragon, spew fire.

Heartsight

It started in a curio shop when my fiancée, Deirdre, leaned across too near my face to reach for an item on the top shelf as I turned to say something to her. Her arm and my face came together at eye level, and my glasses flew off. They landed several feet away on a concrete floor. "Oh, sorry, Will," Deirdre said, giggling.

We could see that one of the lenses was broken in several places. Deidre stopped giggling. I'd forgotten to bring my backup pair, and we were on vacation several time zones from home. And, I NEED those glasses. *"Well there goes this vacation. It could be a week or longer before I can get new eyeglasses.... Wait! I can use the unbroken lens to see enough to get around. It'll look funny, but maybe this trip isn't ruined after all."*

Just then, a harried father chased a two-year-old around a corner into the aisle my glasses had crashed into. It was like watching a train wreck in slow motion. I tried to yell, "STOP!" but the other lens was crushed by the father's foot before I got half the word out. *"Well, that's it! Now I'm officially screwed!"*

The owner of the shop saw what happened and rushed over to me. "Do you have a spare pair?"

I shook my head.

"Well, I think I have a pair that will work for you. I'll be right back."

He shuffled into the back room and came out with a pair of glasses unlike any I'd seen before.

Thinking they must be nonprescription reading glasses, I held up my hand and said, "I'm sorry but those won't work. I have poor vision in both eyes; I'm nearsighted; and reading glasses won't help."

He smiled patiently. "Please, try them on."

I did, and to my amazement, I could see perfectly with both lenses—better in fact than I had been able to with my glasses before they broke.

"See? Give your eyes a little time to adjust to these lenses, and you'll see better than you ever did."

"What a lucky thing that you had glasses with lenses that worked perfectly for both my eyes. Incredible. I'm grateful to you. How much do I owe you?"

He smiled again with kind crinkling eyes, slanted his head slightly, and said, "No charge. They were meant for you. I only ask the same thing of you that the one who gave them to me asked of me: 'When you no longer need them, give them to someone who does.'"

I couldn't believe my good fortune. "Certainly! I'll be happy to do that. Thank you for your kindness and generosity."

He bowed his head slightly forward and to the side and said, "Enjoy the rest of your day and your lives."

Deirdre and I thought that was an odd thing to say, and for that matter, he was an odd little man, but we were glad to have met him.

We continued our vacation and were having fun, but something else happened that was quite odd. The longer I wore the glasses, the better I could *see* people. Not just their exterior features; it was as though, when I looked into someone's eyes, I could see into their heart.

It got to the point where I could tell whether I'd be treated kindly by a stranger or whether a taxi driver planned to overcharge us by taking the long route to our destination. I couldn't read their minds, just their hearts; but, seeing the latter gave me great insight as to what their actions would be.

I didn't mention this to Deirdre. I didn't want her thinking I was going crazy. But, after a couple of days, I couldn't hold back any longer. She, of course, didn't believe me, so we played a game where I'd predict the way someone would treat us or how they would act. Then, we observed what actually happened. When they were gone, we discussed the whole thing. I was right over and over again just by seeing into their hearts.

She was a hard sell, but after a couple more days, Deirdre believed I really could see into people's hearts. Then, yet another strange thing happened. At first, I thought I was imagining it but quickly realized it wasn't my imagination. Deirdre had stopped looking into my eyes. I tried various things to get her to look directly at me, but she wouldn't.

Finally, frustrated, I blurted out, "Why won't you look at me anymore?"

"You're imagining things! Of course, I look at you." But, even then, it was barely a sideways glance.

"Please! LOOK AT ME!"

She turned and stared straight into my eyes. I knew immediately why she had avoided it. Her eyes told me her heart's secret. It only took a heartbeat to rip mine out of my chest and crush it under the staggering weight of truth. She was in love with someone else. I closed my eyes and shook my head. *"NO! It can't be."* But, her expression removed all doubt.

We ended our vacation early. There was little need for discussion. I knew all I needed to know with that one look in her eyes. We had no future together, and there was no reason to prolong our goodbye.

When I got home, I told my friends and family the wedding was canceled. Whenever I didn't have to go to work, I hid in my apartment to attempt to heal a heart that seemed far beyond repair. I hated the day I put on those glasses but was eternally grateful I'd worn them. I needed to learn the truth, but it felt like, instead of setting me free, it was killing me.

One day, I realized it had been a long time since I'd looked into my own eyes. It was with some trepidation that I looked in the mirror. I was pleasantly surprised I liked what I saw. Mostly. I immediately put more focus on being kinder.

About a month later, I answered a knock on the door. It was someone I recognized as a new neighbor whom I'd seen a few times in the parking lot and on the walkway.

"Hi, I'm Grace. I moved in next door while you were gone. Mrs. Roberts mentioned you weren't feeling well so I thought I'd make some homemade chicken soup. It's guaranteed to help make you feel better."

"Thank you, Grace." I looked into her eyes and loved what I saw. I knew then my heart would heal. "Please come in."

The "Misunderstanding"

The trip had been grueling. Like most of the rest of the crowd, Ray Johnson was tired and getting impatient. Watching the endless stream of suitcases on the over-stuffed carousel, he marveled at the similarity of the bags: black with the same design and shape. He found Jan's bag and the one for their five-year-old daughter Grace. *"Now where's mine? Ah, there it is!"* He grabbed it but was interrupted by his wife as he bent to check the name on the tag.

"Jayce and Vickie are nearly out front. Let's go before they have to drive around the airport again."

The Kendalls were long-time close friends. After brief hugs and greetings, the luggage was loaded, and the trip home was full of stories about their daughter's first trip to Disneyland.

The Kendalls helped unload the baggage, said goodnight, and drove away when the phone in the Johnsons' house rang. Ray muttered, handed off the sleepy Grace to Jan, fumbled for his keys, and barely reached the phone in time. "This is Ray."

"Ray Johnson?"

"Yes."

"YOU STOLE MY BAG AND I WANT IT BACK!"

"What are you talking about?"

"AT THE AIRPORT! YOU'RE DEAD IF YOU OPENED OR TOOK ANYTHING FROM IT!"

"Whoa! I don't take kindly to threats. You want to calm down?"

"NO! I WANT MY SUITCASE!

"Hang on a minute. Let me check the suitcases. Did you have a ribbon tied to it?"

"Yeah. A ribbon with playing cards."

"Uh oh, I tied the same kind of ribbon on mine. Hang on, let me check. What's your name?"

"Billy Burdett. Yeah, go check, BUT YOU BETTER NOT OPEN IT!"

Ray set the phone down, grabbed the suitcase, checked the name on the ID tag and sighed.

"I have your bag. I'm sorry; I must have taken yours by mistake. Do you have mine?"

"Yes."

"It's late. I'll be happy to meet you at the airport tomorrow morning to swap our bags."

"NO. *I'M COMIN' NOW!* REMEMBER, YOU'RE DEAD IF YOU OPEN IT."

The line went dead.

Ray held the phone a moment, trying to fight back panic and figure out what to do. "Jan, take Grace to a neighbor's and stay there."

"Why? What's wrong?"

"Some nutcase is coming here. I accidentally grabbed his bag at the airport. He made threats. It's probably nothing, but just in case, I want the two of you out of the house when he comes."

"Call the cops!"

"I will. As soon as you're safe. Hurry."

"Come with us."

"No! If I go, it'll just make him madder. I want this resolved tonight. Don't worry; the cops will probably get here before he does."

Jan scooped up Grace and kissed her husband. "Be careful!"

"I will."

Ray watched until they were safely inside the neighbors' house, then called the cops. He told them the situation and was told units were on their way. He went to his safe, but his hands were shaking so much it took three tries to unlock it. Ray pulled out and loaded a 12-gauge shotgun and .357 Magnum revolver. He didn't want trouble, but this whacko scared him. He wanted to be prepared and able to defend himself. Ray wasn't a great shot, but, with a shotgun at close range, he wouldn't miss no matter how scared he was.

Ray brought Burdett's bag to the front door and jotted down the man's name and address in case he left before the cops arrived. He placed the guns so they'd be out of sight but within reach. *"Come on, cops! Get here!"*

He jumped when pounding on the door sounded like a battering ram was being used.

"I'M HERE, PISS-ANT! GIVE ME MY BAG OR I'LL BREAK YOUR SCRAWNY NECK!"

A couple of police cruisers screeched to a halt, and two cops rushed to the front door. Ray watched through the peephole and could hear through the door. Although Burdett weighed at least forty pounds more than the two cops combined, his tone and demeanor immediately changed as soon as they arrived. "Good evening, officers. It's all a misunderstanding. This person and I accidentally grabbed each other's bags at the airport. When I tried to get mine, this Johnson fella threatened me." Burdett knocked again, this time rather gently. Ray opened the door and the suitcases were quickly exchanged.

"He was the one who threatened..." Ray spluttered.

"STOP!" The taller cop, a sergeant named Murphy, cut him off. "It's one man's word against the other, so I'm warning both of you: This better be the end of it. You both have your own bags back. No more threats from either of you. Do you both understand?"

Burdett nodded.

Ray was so furious he could barely speak but managed to say "Okay."

Burdett asked, "Can I go now?"

"Yeah."

"Sorry for this little misunderstanding." Burdett smiled and left.

"May we come in, Mr. Johnson?"

"Please." He pointed to a couch. "Have a seat."

"I'm Sergeant Murphy and this is Officer Trowden. On the way over here, we checked the record of the man you said threatened you. William 'Billy' Burdett has a long rap sheet. Mostly violent crimes. To our knowledge, he hasn't done anything lately and isn't wanted for anything. We could have brought him downtown, but since it was your word against his, he'd have been released before we walked back to our squad cars and angrier than ever. Burdett is a violent and vengeful man. Holds grudges a long time. We hope our warning scared him off, but, just in case, we'll request extra patrols on your street for a while."

"Thank you, sergeant."

"Be careful with this guy. He's dangerous and doesn't make idle threats. Please call us right away if he contacts you again."

"Will do."

— —

A week passed. The Johnsons had a home security alarm installed, but, otherwise, the incident began to fade away in their minds.

One bright morning after Ray left for work, Jan opened their automatic garage door and loaded Grace into her car seat. As she stood up, a hand viciously grabbed her hair and yanked her around. Jan cried out in pain and fear. She was looking at the lower chest of a huge man. He thrust his hulking frame against her so hard she gasped and crashed against the car's door frame.

"MOMMY!" Grace sobbed.

The man clamped a massive hand over Jan's mouth, leaned down and brushed his lips against her ear. She felt his hot breath and the rough whiskers of a days'-old beard. His voice was deep and gravelly but he whispered so softly she had to strain to hear. "Make a sound and she dies. Understand?" She quickly nodded. He unclamped her mouth.

"I'm okay, Grace. We're just talking."

The brute whispered, "Gotta message for your piss-ant husband: Tell him I tried to settle this man to man, but he called the cops. Do it again and you and your daughter will die. Slowly."

Burdett rubbed his rough hand against her face. "Tell him he'll see me again. Soon." He slapped her so hard her face felt on fire, her ears rang, blood trickled from her nose, and tears filled her eyes. "That's a love tap compared to what I'll do to you and your girl if the cops are called again." He laughed, a wicked laugh that got louder and deeper as he walked away.

— —

Jayce Kendall answered his home office phone. "It's Ray. Jan's nearly hysterical. That psychopath I told you about last week just attacked her in our garage. He threatened to kill Jan and Grace if I call the cops again. I'm headed home, but I'm at least thirty minutes away."

"I'll be there in ten."

"Thank you! Bring a gun. The guy is huge and violent."

Jayce grabbed a pistol as he ran to his car. The weapon was

already loaded.

By the time Ray arrived, Jayce had calmed Jan down; but Ray was livid. When he was sure Jan and Grace were okay, he motioned for Jayce to join him in the den. "I'm going to have to track down and kill that sonuvabitch! My family won't be safe until he's dead!"

"That's what he *wants* you to do so he can ambush you on his turf. Then when he kills you it will be self-defense. Plus, think about your family."

"I *am* thinking about them!"

"No. I mean, even if you kill him, you'll end up in prison for murder. How will you being in prison help them?"

Ray raised balled fists over his bowed head and snarled, "What do you *want* me to do? Wait until he kills me and my family?"

"No. I want you all to stay with Vickie and me for a couple days. These things have a way of working themselves out."

Ray doubted that anything would fix the mess he was in, but he agreed to stay at the Kendalls'. He grabbed a couple of guns while Jan packed some clothes, and they hurried over to their friends' home, being very careful they weren't followed.

— —

Billy Burdett lived in a secluded trailer at the end of a dirt road. At 9:15 p.m., he drained his beer while watching the game and went to the fridge to get another. Burdett slammed the door when he realized it had been his last brew. He swore, kicked the offending fridge, grabbed his keys, and headed the fifty feet to his yellow pickup. Halfway there, a man stepped out of the shadows and stood about four paces in front of him. Burdett stopped.

"Who the hell are you and waddya want?"

"I'm the man who's going to help make sure you never bother Ray and

Jan Johnson again."

Burdett's laughter came out a roar. "YOU AND WHAT ARMY?" He took a step toward the intruder, relishing the pain he was about to inflict.

"This one." Jayce whistled. Eighteen men stepped out of the darkness, creating a circle around Jayce and the brute. "I'd like you to meet a few of our friends, relatives, and teammates."

Shocked, Burdett stopped and looked around. He knew he could take out several of them but nowhere near all of them. As though a switch had been flipped, his tone and demeanor became friendly. "I think there must be some misunderstanding."

"Yeah, Ray said you'd probably say that."

Silence.

Jayce turned his head to the right and yelled toward the shadows. "Hey, Ray. Gotta minute?" Ray showed himself and walked to Jayce.

Jayce continued, "Well Burdett, you have exactly one chance to correct this 'misunderstanding' by confessing everything you did and apologizing to Ray for it."

"Hell no. I'm not sayin'..."

"That was your chance!" Twenty men moved as one toward Burdett.

"WAIT!" The men stopped. "Okay. I threatened you and your family."

"And grabbed my wife's hair, slammed and trapped her against her car, and slapped her."

Burdett looked at the faces of the men in the circle looking for lack of resolve or weakness. All he saw was rage.

He whispered, "Yes."

"What was that?"

"YES! I'm sorry! Okay? I promise to leave you and your family alone."

Jayce laughed, "You're not getting off that easy." Several men pulled out their phones and played back Burdett's confessions. "We all decided the climate here is bad for your health. It's time you left the state and never came back. Tonight."

"WHAT?"

Twenty men moved closer.

"OKAY! I'll go."

"You've got thirty minutes to clear out."

Burdett headed for his trailer. The men watched him like hawks to make sure he didn't try anything.

On a hunch, Jayce searched the yellow pickup. Sure enough, he found a loaded gun under the driver's seat.

Twenty-seven minutes after Burdett started packing, he was in his truck and ready to go.

"We'll follow you 'til you cross the state line. Then the cops get your confession."

Burdett floored the old pickup and roared out in a cloud of dust with carloads full of men on his tail.

Jayce turned to Ray as they watched them go. "It looks like it's over, my friend!"

Ray let out a big sigh. "Yes. Thank you! I owe you all a lot. Especially you."

"That's what friends are for."

They smiled, gave each other a bear hug, and Ray left to pick up his family and take them home. He couldn't wait to tell Jan the good news.

— —

Burdett crossed the state line and the men in the other cars turned and headed home. A few miles down the highway Burdett stopped in a small in the woods to take a leak. He was furious he'd been run out of town, and shouted, "I'm going to kill that whole family!"

— —

Two hours later, state trooper Moe Burnside noticed a yellow pickup in a clearing in the woods slightly off the highway. He saw a beat-up yellow pick-up. It looked abandoned. He called in the plates. The reply made him reach for his gun, call for backup, and approach very carefully. He always did when suspects were as dangerous as William Burdett's rap sheet indicated he was.

No need. What was left of Burdett's head dangled out the driver's side window frame. Blood was everywhere. The trooper flashed his light inside the truck and saw a very dead suspect with a gun clutched in his right hand. He sighed. *"Suicide."*

Seventy-five miles away, Jayce Kendall's brain roiled. He'd followed the caravan, kept going when the others turned back, and stopped out of sight when Burdett pulled into the clearing in the woods. Kendall knew Burdett would never leave his friends alone. The psychopath's fate was sealed when he heard Burdett screaming about killing them. He crept to the open passenger side window of the old yellow truck.

Burdett saw him and growled, "YOU'RE DEAD!" as he reached for his gun under the seat.

"Looking for this?"

When Burdett looked up, Jayce leaned in, pressed the muzzle of Burdett's gun against the man's temple, and fired. It was the only way he could be sure Burdett would never have another "misunderstanding" with Ray and his family, or anyone else, again.

Jayce wiped his prints from the gun and placed it in Burdett's hand to make sure the psychopath's prints were where they needed to be. He arranged Burdett's hand and gun to make it look like he'd shot himself.

— —

Returning to his car, Jayce stripped the surgeon's gloves from his hands and placed them inside-out in a pocket. About half-way home, he bought a meal from a fast-food joint. He ate it in his car, stuffed the gloves inside the empty bag, wadded it up, and threw it into a garbage can before leaving the parking lot.

Jayce knew no one could ever learn what he'd done. He alone would carry the secret burden for the rest of his days.

Here

An older, distinguished-looking man met me at the boat. He had an honest and friendly face. I guessed he was a senior executive at the company. I grabbed my suitcase and he extended his hand to help me out of the small boat. The invitation said to expect the interview process to be as long as three days and they would provide food and lodging during that time.

"Welcome Ron! I'm Charlie. Was the boat ride okay?"

"Yes."

"Good. Please come with me. We'll get you situated."

I felt like I was in paradise. We walked up a lushly landscaped walkway into the lobby of what appeared to be a high-end private resort hotel. I noticed he treated the resort staffers with respect yet in a friendly, casual manner, and they did the same with him. It appeared everyone was on a first-name basis.

"Are you hungry, Ron?"

I nodded and smiled.

"Good! A delicious banquet awaits us, but first let's get you to your suite and give you a chance to freshen up after your long flight and boat ride. Then we have a little paperwork..."

Twenty minutes after being shown to my suite, I met Charlie in a quiet lounge. It was tropically-themed and even had some live colorful birds on stands scattered around the room. We sat in a corner, which I assumed was so we could quietly conduct business.

Charlie handed me a single sheet of paper that immediately recognized as a Non-Disclosure Agreement but it was unlike any NDA I'd ever seen before. It wasn't full of legalese, and essentially said that whatever I experience Here must stay Here and that I must never mention any aspect of my visit Here to anyone who isn't an employee of Here nor any aspect of any process, system, or operation Here. I thought it was an odd document, especially the way the word "Here" was capitalized, but I consider myself an honest fellow and under the circumstances didn't see any harm in the terms, so signed and returned it to Charlie.

"Wonderful!" He folded and pocketed the document. "Let's eat!" he said motioning toward the banquet room. The meal was delicious.

After the feast we adjourned to Charlie's office. "Are you enjoying your stay so far, Ron?"

"Very much so!"

"Good! I believe you are going to experience many pleasant surprises during your visit. Before I begin asking you questions, I'd like to give you the opportunity to ask whatever you like, so fire away!"

"Thank you, Charlie. I am curious about a number of things. First, where are we?"

Charlie laughed. "Ah one of the hardest questions first! We're Here."

"Here?"

"Yes, Here. Here is an island that was bought from a friendly government by a trust that was set up by a couple of multi-billionaires. They left a huge endowment for the trust, and have done something similar in a few other places around the world."

"Why?"

"The billionaires were as old as they were rich. They were not pleased by the direction the world was headed in, so they devised several social experiments hoping they could foster better ways for people to live and work with each other. Here is one of those experimental communities."

"Amazing! How come I've never heard of Here or any of the other places?"

"It was decided that the experiments must be kept secret. I believe you will soon figure out on your own as to why that is necessary."

"You use past tense when mentioning the billionaires. Are they dead?"

"Yes. Sadly, they died before seeing any of the communities they envisioned come to fruition."

"Who were they?"

"I'm sorry, Ron. They wished to remain anonymous and that was a condition of the very generous endowments they created for Here and elsewhere. They didn't do it for further fame or glory. Here is just one of the seeds they planted in the hope that all of humanity will one day be able to taste new and delicious fruit. The endowments allow for very generous annual budgets for Here."

"Who runs everything Here?"

"We do."

"Who's we? Is there a boss or board of directors?"

"Everyone who chooses to participate in Here has an equal say in every aspect of Here."

"What? How can that function? Every place needs leaders, Charlie."

"We're all leaders Here. We just lead different things. And we're all followers."

"Somebody has got to make decisions."

"We all do, Ron."

"Huh? HOW?"

"We all own an equal piece in all the assets of the trust and have an equal seay in all decisions via daily votes. We of course don't all vote our share every time. We vote when an issue is important to us or when we have some knowledge about the question at hand. Each Stakeholder Here can track all issues important to him or her, and if we don't like the results of a vote, we can have another vote in an attempt to change the result. That way it doesn't pay for anyone to try to slip in things that could harm us. Our rights are guaranteed by the trust. It is like our Constitution."

"What kind of government do you have?"

"We the people are the only government we have or need."

"What about a judicial system?"

"All Stakeholders are the judges and vote the results like juries do elsewhere, but everyone Here can vote in a trial. For that reason, we need no juries."

"Who makes the laws?"

"The trust by-laws are the only laws needed Here."

"Those by-laws most be many volumes long."

"On the contrary, Ron. We really only have one law, and it is sufficient."

"One law? What single law could possibly be so all-encompassing?"

"Our law is to be kind. You'd be surprised as to the multitude of situations being kind covers."

"What about disputes between neighbors?"

"They are very rare. When they occur, the parties bring their stories to Stakeholders Here. Everyone interested determines via vote what the kindest approach to handling the issue is, and that is what is done."

"That must make the lawyers unhappy!"

"We have no lawyers, nor need for them."

"What about police? Prisons? Jails? Courts?"

"We have no need for them. If a person is unwilling or unable to be kind, their share in the trust can revoked by a vote of all Stakeholders Here, and since only Stakeholders are able to live on this trust-owned island, they must leave Here and not return."

"Does that often happen?"

"Thankfully, it is very rare. We attempt to be very careful as to those who are invited to come Here, and when people come they nearly always want to stay."

"So losing one's stake Here is a little like being stripped of one's citizenship?"

"Something like that. But it's not the reason people are kind Here. They're kind because they're surrounded by kindness. It's a way of life. A natural reaction to kindness is to be kind. It's a virtuous circle."

"That makes sense!"

"We think so."

"What do politicians do here, Charlie?"

"We have no politicians."

"That sounds wonderful!"

"We've found that politicians tend to be counterproductive to what the people want."

"What about medical care?"

"We have some of the best medical outcomes of anywhere in the world."

"That must hugely expensive."

"All basic healthcare is free Here. We've found it is better for Stakeholders Here to help people stay healthy than constantly be trying to cure preventable and very expensive-to-treat diseases."

"So Here must be one of those places where to become a member you've got to give up all your worldly possessions, right?"

"Just the opposite, Ron. We neither want nor need your money. If you decide to join us you'll be able to do whatever you want with your assets.

Some people leave them in investments elsewhere just in case their stay Here doesn't suit them. Others give all their assets away. Others bring their assets but quickly find they are worthless Here."

"Worthless, Charlie? How can that be?"

"We have no currency, in the normal sense, nor need of one. We all have a decent house to live in."

"But what happens if someone wants more? A bigger, fancier house and nicer furniture? How can one earn such things?"

"Well first, with our basic food, clothing, medical, education, and housing needs covered at such nice levels, many people are perfectly satisfied with them."

"But you haven't answered my question, Charlie."

"Patience, my friend. I was just getting to that part. People can certainly obtain such things Here, but they don't "earn" them in the normal sense. They are indirectly given to them."

"There you go again, evading my question."

"Not at all, for you see, every person Here is given a thousand Appreciation Credits per year to use however they want, *except* on themselves and their immediate family."

"Except...?"

"Yes. Stakeholders Here find others who are especially kind, pleasant, cheerful, productive, helpful, conscientious, diligent, etc, and reward them with Appreciation Credits. In that way, the people Here who are the most beneficial and appreciated are also rewarded for their extra efforts."

"Wow! I could see how that could incentivize people who want more than the basics. Is my suite an example of basic living accommodations?"

"Yes. The basic standard of living is very high Here. No one lives in poverty."

"So from what I've seen of the basics so far they do indeed appear to be quite nice. Can the Appreciation Credits one receives from others Here be used for sending children to college?"

"That's not necessary. Quality education is free Here. We all win when everyone's potential is unleashed by a high quality education. But educations are earned Here. One's quality of education is in direct relation to one's effort and demonstrated results. It isn't a free ride."

"Speaking of free rides, how do you handle freeloaders Here, Charlie?"

"That's simple. We have none. To take without giving would be unkind and as I mentioned earlier one must be kind to remain a stakeholder Here. Everyone is free to pursue their passions so long as their passions don't harm others and do contribute Here in some way. We've found that when people do what they love, they do it eagerly and tend to do it well. Nearly all people, if given the choice of doing what they love that is also beneficial to others, or doing nothing and sitting at home, will ultimately do what they love. We help them find ways to do what they love that will also help Here."

"But what about jobs that are so boring or dirty that no one wants to do them?"

"Excellent question! We've been able to automate a lot of them. For the rest, many people help out with the worst tasks to lighten the load of such jobs. Additionally people who choose to do those jobs and do them well and cheerfully tend to get rewarded very well in Appreciation Credits by everyone else. For example, janitors, busboys, dishwashers, and the like are often some of the best "compensated" folks Here."

"No wonder they all seem so happy, Charlie."

"Being respected, valued, and compensated for a job well done can go a long way toward happiness."

"What about taxes? Let me guess, you don't need them Here, right?"

"Right. And each Stakeholder gets to vote on how the money from the endowment is spent each year. We add up the votes for the various potential budget items and prorate expenditures based on the votes, so we never go over budget, and every Stakeholder knows their votes truly count Here. In fact we not only don't go over budget, we often have a sizable surplus. Many Stakeholders vote to hold back some of their spending proration for reserves in case in some future years something may come up that would require more than the endowment payout for that year. We want to ensure we always have enough for a given year because we cannot touch the principal in the trust, only the annual payout amounts."

"It's clear no one is forced to come. Can anyone leave at any time?"

"Of course! By the way, I'll bet you've figured out by now why we try to keep Here a secret."

"You probably don't want to be overrun by tens of thousands of people trying to immediately move Here, right."

Charlie smiled and nodded. "Exactly!"

"So how does one get invited to become a Stakeholder?"

"We watch for people who are especially kind, help others, and have skills we need. People like you, Ron. Are you interested?"

"I've never been more interested in anything in my life. How soon can I start?"

Desperation

Jacob Stevens wiped the dust-filled sweat from his face as he stared down the bank into the long, muddy puddle. His thoughts raced back to a time when this ugly gouge in parched earth had been a beautiful river running through verdant grazing land. For sixteen years, the rains had been plentiful, feeding the river and swelling his herd. His long-time friend, Ron Parker, owned the land on the other side of the river. They'd helped each other build successful ranches and large herds. It was a peaceful and prosperous time.

Then, the most severe drought either rancher had ever experienced hit.

The first year caused few problems.

By the second dry year, the river was noticeably narrower and shallower. He and Jacob's wife Janice became concerned. Their three children were counting on them. But there was still plenty of water to go around, and it would begin to rain soon, or so they hoped.

It didn't. The "rainy" season in the third year of drought brought little more than a few scattered days of sprinkles, most of which quickly evaporated in the warmer-than-usual temperatures.

Jacob and Ron eyed the river apprehensively as it continued to shrink. At first, they talked about it and worried together. They tried to trim their herds by selling some of their cattle, but all those good years had swollen herds for several hundred miles in all directions and glutted the market. Prices plunged. They had a choice of selling off their herds at huge losses and virtually starting over after twenty years of hard work, or holding on and hoping the drought would end. They did the only thing that made sense to them at the time. They held on.

They guessed wrong. The fourth year was hotter and drier than the first three. When the heat grew more punishing and the river continued to wither, so did their conversations. Their friendship wilted. It became apparent that if both herds kept drinking from what was left of the river, neither herd would survive. The families of both men needed those herds and that water.

The bellows of Jacob's thirsty herd underscored the problem. Another cow collapsed and couldn't get up. They would all die of thirst unless something drastic was done—and soon.

A horse whinnied on the other bank of the slim mudhole that had once been a river. Jacob quickly looked across to see Ron Parker astride his horse, looking grim-faced at the puddle, and then at him.

They stared at each other, knowing what must be done, but neither wanting to do it. It was far too late for either man to move his herd and no place to take them. It was too late for anything but spilling blood. As the sun began to set, they nodded grimly.

The shots rang out and echoed for miles.

— —

Two hundred miles away, unseasonably early rain clouds were forming. Huge, dark, swollen masses would arrive overnight and pour an inch of rain onto the parched ranches. It was the beginning of what would prove to be a very wet season.

— —

It was after midnight, but Jacob was still awake, lying in bed, troubled by what he'd done. He couldn't believe it when he heard the first drops of rain on his roof. He quietly put on his boots and went outside, letting the cool rain drench him. He felt great joy, but it was followed by sadness about what had happened earlier that day. Soaking up the rain, he thought back to that bloody sundown...

— —

Jacob stared at Ron and said, "Seems we have a choice: draw on each other or begin shooting our own herds so some of each herd might survive."

Ron nodded.

They faced each other and drew their pistols. Both hesitated. Then Ron turned and killed one of his weakest cows.

The slaughter lasted until both had emptied their six-shooters. Neither had the stomach for more killing that day and had used the oncoming darkness as an excuse to wait until the morning to continue the heart-wrenching job...

— —

Now, standing in mud and pelted by raindrops, Jacob thought of Ron and smiled. Their families, friendship, and nearly all of their remaining cattle would survive for another day.

The Best Policy

Gabriel and Willow Johnson had worked hard all their lives. Now in their early seventies, they wanted to retire from farming, sell their property, and live the rest of their lives traveling the country. They'd even discussed it with two local real-estate firms, but the valuations they'd been quoted were far below what they thought they needed and what the property had been worth only a few years ago. It seemed their timing couldn't have been worse. They decided not to list their property.

A drought hit California hard, and their well was nearly dry. They could no longer water their meager crops. Their land was on the coast, but other than the sizable piece of land their small house was on, the rest of the property was broken up into little fingers of land that jutted out into the ocean. It didn't have pretty views, and state laws forbade the building of additional homes in that area. They figured they'd probably end up dying in the lonely old house.

On a scorching mid-July afternoon, a man drove down their dusty road, got out of his car, and knocked on their door.

Gabriel opened the door and saw a pleasant man of medium build, who wore a business suit and a big smile. He said, "Hi, I'm Quinn Davison and I came here to see if you might be willing to talk about selling your land."

"Please come in and have a seat," Gabriel said, motioning him to a chair.

"Would you like some lemonade after your long drive, Mr. Davison?" Willow offered.

"I'd love some, ma'am," he replied. She went to the kitchen and returned with a tall glass. He drank it down to half a glass in one long swallow. "Thank you! Whew, it's sure hot today and this is mighty tasty."

Not one for small talk, Gabriel got down to business. "We might be interested in selling, but first, there are some things about the property you should know. You can't build on much of the land, and our well may run dry if we have another drought year." Telling the whole truth and not hiding important information was the way Gabriel and Willow had always done things. They weren't about to change now, no matter how badly they wanted to move and see the country while they were still healthy enough to enjoy it. Gabriel added, "Now, do you still want to discuss buying our property?"

The stranger looked at them, paused as if he were making a decision, and said, "I appreciate your integrity, Mr. and Mrs. Johnson. Your honesty is as refreshing as this lemonade. I was prepared to be somewhat evasive with you as to what we plan to do with the property and to try to negotiate as low a price from you as possible, but you've been straight with me, so I'll be straight with you. With the drought, this state badly needs fresh water. We plan to build a large de-salinization plant and believe your property is ideal for our needs. For those reasons, and in no small part because of your honesty, I'm willing to offer top dollar for your property." He wrote a figure on a piece of paper. "How does this price sound?"

— —

A month later, Gabriel and Willow were on the road in the RV of their dreams, headed for the sights they'd longed for a lifetime to see.

Hoodwinked

Rancher Cal Johnson looked at the land sale paperwork and smiled. *"You sure hoodwinked that city boy,"* he thought to himself. Ever since Karma Creek had nearly dried up, the land around it had become virtually worthless for raising cattle or any other livestock or crops. There was no other water for many miles, and the water in the creek wouldn't have supported more than a couple dozen head. *"I was lucky to find such a sucker to buy it. That foolish city boy Michael Krumholz is going to lose his shirt."* The thought brought another smile to his face.

Forty-five minutes later, Michael Krumholz stood in Karma Creek. He reached down and pulled up a handful of wet soil. As the water drained beneath his fingers, it lightly washed away a thin film that had covered flakes and even some small nuggets that glistened brightly in the golden sunlight. The view made geological engineer Michael Krumholz smile.

Everyone Wins

It was six degrees below zero Fahrenheit on Koldon – tourist season, the warmest time of year. Travelers came from around the galaxy to experience "The Snow Planet" and its unique wildlife and other attributes. Visitor Scott Kanemoto and his guide Tierdo huddled near a heat cell at the end of a long and satisfying day spent capturing images of creatures he'd long dreamed of seeing.

They drank a heated alcoholic beverage called xinthe. It had a strong earthy taste and a powerful kick.

"What do you make this stuff out of?"

"Trust me. You do not want to know!" Tierdo laughed so hard he almost fell over.

Feeling no pain, Kanemoto decided to ask a question that many around the galaxy often wondered about this planet. "It is said that, on colder evenings, it is the custom of your planet to, uh, loan your female mate to visitors to help keep your guest warm at night. Is that true?"

Once again, Tierdo laughed uncontrollably, rocking back and forth so far his ears almost touched the frozen ground with each swing. "Can you keep a secret, my friend?"

Scott nodded.

"We used to do that long ago when the first visitors arrived. It didn't work out very well for anybody. Guests didn't know how to behave during such sacred rituals. It cost some visitors their lives. Have you noticed that our females remain out of sight when male visitors are present?"

The guest nodded again.

"Though we still honor our traditions and our guests by offering a female to help warm the bed of our guests, it is never our female mate. It is safer for our guests and mates. We don't mention that to visitors because we do not wish to appear rude.

"We share our expectations of how guests should treat our females, and warn them of the consequences if our traditions aren't honored.

"You weren't offered a female for the simple reason that none are with us on our journey.

"Females who warm the bed of a guest have no mate and wish a warmer bed for themselves—and perhaps something more. They are held in high esteem and often very good at giving, and getting, something more.

"In that way, everyone wins."

The Elm Street Ladies' Club

The thirteen little old ladies on Elm Street were more than a little unusual. They wore bright blue hats and played bridge at picnic tables at the Elm Street Park instead of inside their homes as most people of their advanced ages and infirmaries do.

Sadly, their neighborhood had become rundown over the years, and crime increased. That didn't stop them from playing cards in the park instead of behind locked doors.

One bright sunny day, the inevitable happened. A grungy-looking man in his early twenties walked up to Myriam and demanded, "Give me your purse!"

She just smiled and firmly said, "No! If you take it you'll deal with our club!"

"I'm not afraid of you old biddies!" He grabbed her purse and began to run. Myriam's friend, Mabel flung her cane at his legs. He tripped and fell but clung to Myriam's purse.

The thug scrambled to his feet and flicked open a switchblade knife. "Guess I'm going to have to show you a lesson or two about who you're dealing with!" He turned toward Gwen who was trapped in her wheel chair.

He felt a tap on his shoulder from behind and wheeled around.

Touched

"You've met us ladies, now meet our club!" yelled Kate as she swung the 32-ounce, 32-inch metal baseball bat straight for his head.

That club was the last thing he saw for a very long time.

Fool's Gold

Clem Maxwell rushed into the Dirty Dog Saloon and came to an abrupt stop when he heard her voice. It was the sweetest he'd ever heard and came from the most beautiful woman he'd ever seen. Clem had fallen in love the moment he laid eyes on Adeline. Virtually everyone in the nearly all-male gold-mining town had done the same. Clem and the rest of the men had been lonely for so long that if she'd sung like a banshee and looked like a filly they probably still would have fallen in love. The fact that Adeline sang like a songbird and was truly beautiful made her all the more irresistible.

Clem eased toward the bar, never taking his eyes off Adeline. He felt a tap on the shoulder and turned to see Slim Deets. They'd been close friends until Adeline had come to town. "Why you low life sonuvab..."

"Now, Clem, don't you go sayin' something we're both gonna regret. I only went on a picnic with her."

"But you know that Adeline and I are almost engaged."

"I know no such thing. You've only gone for one ride out in the country with her."

"But we rode together before you had a picnic with her."

"Come on, Clem, let me buy you a drink." Slim poured enough gold dust on the bar for several drinks.

"No!" Clem brushed the dust off the bar onto the floor behind it with the back of his hand. "I'm not drinkin' with the man who tried to steal my girl."

Behind the bar, Red Benton was thrilled. *"Poor fools."* This was the third time today a similar scene had played out with other men, and, each time, he'd swept up and pocketed the gold dust.

Red had many doubts when Adeline suggested they go west to raise money to buy a house in Boston. She said gold miners would crave the companionship of a beautiful woman at least as much as they needed picks and shovels. He finally admitted she was right. Her plan worked even better than she thought it would. She simply showed up, got a job singing in the best bar in town, and acted like a lady. The only other women in town were a few gap-toothed disease-ridden sad souls who made a living – if you could call it that – on their backs.

Adeline shined like the warm sun in the dark, cold, lonely existence of most miners. They showered her with expensive gifts in their efforts to woo her. To her credit, she told them she was spoken for by someone from Boston but neglected to mention it was the man who'd come to the mining town the day after she did and was now their bartender. It worked best that way and was safer for Red.

Adeline and Red had discussed it early this morning. He said they had enough gold to buy their house in Boston. Adeline wanted to stay a bit longer but agreed to leave on tomorrow's noon stage.

Adeline was indeed planning on leaving on the noon stage tomorrow, but not with her fiancé. *"Poor Red. The fool. He still has no clue I've fallen for Jack."* Jack O'Hanlon had struck the Mother Lode and was now a very rich man.

She headed for the only place in town that usually served beef instead of bear or worse. Red was to meet her there in a few minutes. She decided to confess to him at lunch today in such a public place so, hopefully, he couldn't make too much of a scene. *"It'll break his heart, and I'm truly sorry for that, but he can have all the money we saved for the house. Besides, I don't need it. I'm about to be engaged to the richest man around these parts and I'll be able to buy houses all over the world."*

Jack O'Hanlon walked out of the Wells Fargo office. He saw Adeline walk into the Beef and Beans. *"The beautiful greedy young fool. She was a lot of fun to bed and dally with but I'd never marry a woman who'd dump her fiancé simply because she found someone richer. There are* always *richer men."* He shook his head and boarded the noon stage.

The Patsy

"These lonely old ladies are such patsies." Carlton Fitzgerald smiled wickedly to himself. *"They're all the same. Flash a smile, listen to their boring sob stories, flash some fancy brochures about some non-existent gold mines, lie about how another little old lady got rich investing in the same mines, talk them into giving their life savings to you in cash so they 'won't have to deal with those greedy IRS agents,' then split."* This was the fourth little old lady he'd bilked in the last two months. *"It's almost like shooting fish in a barrel, only easier."* He gloated.

He flashed his best "You can trust me" smile as she held the large bag of cash, hesitating. Her hands were shaking.

"But this is all I have. I don't know what I'd do if I lost it." Her voice trembled and was barely audible. The frail woman had to be pushing 90.

"There's nothing to worry about, Martha. I gave you a written guarantee that this gold mine will double your money in less than six months, didn't I? How could I do that unless gold was gushing out of the mines?"

"Well, since I have the written guarantee, I guess it's safe." She held out the old bag. He took it and said, "You won't regret this." He turned toward the door and crashed into all 6' 4" 235 pounds of Detective John Marston who'd been waiting in a bedroom for this moment.

The creep was cuffed and his rights were read to him. Martha smiled.

"Well, John. How'd I do?"

"You did great, Aunt Martha."

"That was fun. Can we do it again sometime?"

For as Long as the Music Plays

It was their first slow dance together. He'd waited a long time for this moment. He looked her in the eyes and said, "I love you."

She leaned toward him and whispered in his ear, "I'll love you for as long as the music plays."

His heart broke a little at her words. He wished the dance would go on forever, but, less than three minutes later, it ended. He looked at her with sad eyes, nodded, and turned to walk away.

She reached for his hand, locked her eyes on his, and whispered, "The music is still playing in my heart."

It kept playing for the rest of their lives.

The Decision

Bob "Bulldog" Webb, CEO of Bulldog Enterprises, couldn't believe what he'd just heard from his VP of Sales, Sterling Dixon. On the eve of the announcement of the biggest contract, by far, to be awarded to a company in their industry all year, Dixon had bragged he was certain they'd already won.

When Bulldog asked him how he could be so certain, the VP bragged, "I wrote the bid based on information I received from a senior executive at the firm.

"YOU DID WHAT? We didn't become the biggest and best supplier in this industry by CHEATING! I'm calling Rawn Global's CEO right now and withdrawing our bid!" He picked up the phone.

"Wait! What's the big deal? Everyone does it. We need this contract. Besides, I'm due for a big bonus when we land the deal."

Bulldog looked up the telephone number and began dialing.

"If you withdraw the bid, I'll quit!"

Bulldog kept dialing. Dixon stormed out of the office.

Ninety seconds later the call was routed to Rawn's CEO. "Karen Kennedy."

"Hi, Karen. This is Bulldog Webb. I'm sorry to do this at such short notice but I'm withdrawing our bid."

"Why? We really liked your offer."

"My VP of Sales—correction, now *ex*-VP of Sales—just admitted to me that he based our bid on info leaked to him from a high level exec at your firm. We don't operate that way."

Kennedy let out a big sigh. "Well, Bulldog, Rawn Global recently decided to take in-house all the work that was being done by companies in your industry. Everyone said your company is the one we should buy and, tomorrow afternoon, you'll receive an offer to buy out your firm at a price I believe you're going to like very much."

The news shocked Bulldog. "But... but..."

Kennedy continued, "We know you built the company from scratch and your employers are like family to you, so we're prepared to offer a five-year no-layoff policy to all your employees."

"That is quite generous."

"There's one more thing, Bulldog. I plan to retire soon. I want you to replace me.

"Several members of our board suggested you. I knew you were qualified, but I needed to see firsthand if you are a man of the highest integrity. We arranged to have the information about the bid leaked to your firm to see how you would handle the situation.

"Your decision made ours easy."

Helping the War Effort

1944 Germany, inside a Munitions Factory

The plant superintendent in a speech at the start of yet another agonizingly long and deadly day for slave laborers from the concentration camps:

"You must work harder and faster to help the war effort or you'll be beaten and killed!"

Several of the enslaved workers smiled inwardly. They were already working as hard and fast as they could to help the war effort. Whenever their overseers were distracted, they put almost no propellant in the tank and artillery shells. Whenever their oppressors fired them, the shells would explode inside the weapons' barrels or German lines. Either way, there would be fewer Nazis to slow the Allied advance and their eventual freedom.

Hope

Henry Penfeld and Jake Jacobson were friends and coworkers. Now on their twenty-minute lunch break, they were a portrait of misery. The men raced the clock to finish lunch as they stared at the giant debt board that took up a whole wall of the cafeteria. The name of everyone who worked there was lit up in bright red lights, along with their personal totals of debts, incomes, and whether they were current on paying their bills. Every company and retail store in the U.S. now had one. The old system of credit scores had been discontinued decades ago. The debt boards were a way to shame anyone who got behind on their bills, and to remind everyone they needed to work harder and longer as their debts climbed.

It had started with implanting electronic chips in debit and credit cards for "security" reasons. From there, it wasn't a huge stretch to eventually convince most people to have the chips implanted in their heads instead. The credit companies said it was for the protection of the borrowers, and they offered incentives for people to authorize having the chips embedded in their brains. The deals were irresistible. It was like having a genie pop out of a bottle to grant wishes.

People with chips became known as "Chippers." Credit was very easy to get for Chippers but almost impossible to obtain for those without them, the so-called "Chipless." Interest rates were lowered to almost nothing for those with the chips, but Chipless borrowers had to pay a minimum of 25% more for even the most credit-worthy. It wasn't long before most people had the chips.

Then laws were passed forcing everyone else who owed money to have chips implanted. "After all," the argument went," why should most debtors have chips and not all of them? It's the only fair thing to do." Since the majority were already Chippers, they supported the new law. Taxes were increased to the point where, with their other debts, most people could barely pay them. Those who owed money to the government were also considered debtors so, in effect, nearly everyone became a Chipper.

The law required interest rates to be variable with no caps. When virtually everyone was as heavily indebted as they and their creditors thought they could handle, almost overnight the creditors jacked up all the interest rates to 25%. Bankruptcies were banned. Incomes stagnated, for why should employers pay more when people stood in long lines for the few jobs that were available?

Hundreds of millions of debt addicts became virtual debt slaves overnight.

The chips could only be removed when the debts were completely repaid. A few people tried to have the chips removed before their debts were paid off. That was cheating. They mysteriously died, slowly and painfully. Word got out. The chips were left alone.

The debt treadmills were cranked up. Borrowers felt they had no choice but to run faster. Average work weeks gradually grew to eighty-two hours and were getting longer every year.

Then, when people thought they couldn't take it anymore, those who were behind on their debt payments started getting headaches. If their debts became current, their headaches went away, but if they didn't catch up, the headaches pounded nonstop. The pain increased if they fell further behind in their debt payments. For the most extreme cases, the pain was carefully kept slightly below the level that would trigger unconsciousness. It made no sense to knock out a motivated worker.

Henry asked, “Did you hear about Stan?”

“No. What happened to him?”

“He had a stroke. He was only 38 years old! Poor bastard had intense headaches for over two years and finally worked himself to death.”

“Maybe he’s the lucky one. At this rate I’ll never get out of debt. I’ve had those payment headaches once and never, ever, want to have another one.” Jake rubbed his temples at the memory.

Henry lowered his eyes a bit, and, in a despondent voice said, “I tried to talk my daughter, Martha, out of getting into debt, but you know how kids are. She thought I was exaggerating about the problems debt causes. They glorify debt in school, and she sees all her peers loading up. She can charge whatever she wants now virtually interest-free on those “teaser” rates, and lenders are even letting her slide on her payments a bit without any pain. They want her good and hooked before they flip the switch.” His eyes moistened as he knew he couldn’t protect her from an addiction that would soon enslave her.

“How did we ever get into such a mess?”

“A little at a time, Jake. A little at a time.

Across the cafeteria, Mimi Watter, Sheri Moon, Yvonne Laettner, and Melody Beckman sat together. They, too, watched the board but saw something no one else appeared to notice. Of the hundreds of names listed, the debt of one had slowly but steadily decreased. It was one of them. At the current debt reduction rate, she’d be debt-free in two weeks. Fifteen months ago, they’d come up with a plan they hoped would help them buy back their freedom. Instead of each of them focusing only on the losing game of trying to reduce their own debts, they agreed to work as a team to help pay down the debt of one of them while the other three kept their debts current. Then when the first teammate became debt-free, their salary wouldn't be eaten up by 25% interest rates and could help get the next teammate out of debt much more quickly. Hopefully in two or three more years, they could all be debt-free.

They looked at the board again; then looked at each other and smiled. Their plan was working!

The Mob

When I was twelve and living outside a small town in Georgia in 1967, I was awakened one night by a commotion in front of my family's house. I looked down from my bedroom window and saw about twenty men wearing white robes and pointed hoods. They were carrying flaming torches. Some had guns. One carried a whip.

"P-Pa!"

"I see 'em. Stay in the house!" Pa walked outside.

I ran downstairs. Ma held Jodilee and stood just inside the front door. I tried to rush past them, but Ma grabbed me and said through gritted teeth, "Your pa said stay inside and that's what you're gonna do!" I felt her trembling as she held me back with her arm.

Pa stood facing the mob. "What do you want?"

The one carrying the whip took an unsteady step forward and pointed it at Pa. He swayed a bit like he'd been drinking. "We heard you stopped some of our boys from beatin' up Matthew Green on his way home from high school. Is that true?"

"Yes. Four on one seemed a little unfair, especially when one of the four had a baseball bat, and the others were holding Matthew down."

"They was just havin' some fun. You've gotten too uppity. Forgot your place. We're here to remind you." He uncoiled his long whip. "Tie him to that tree, boys."

Pa reached behind his back and pulled a pistol out of his belt, aiming it at the man with the whip. "This is loaded but won't stay that way if any of you take another step."

The sheets froze.

Suddenly, we heard heavy steps on our back porch, and the doorknob turned. Ma screamed. Pa turned toward her and the mob surged forward.

BANG! BANG! Two shots went off nearly simultaneously; the first in the back of the house, and the other from behind a tree near Pa. The cowards hiding in white robes froze again. Everyone tried to figure out who shot and who was shot.

"No one's gonna be whipped, 'lessen you want a belly full of lead." Matthew Green's pa stepped out from behind a tree holding a 12-gauge shotgun. He yelled toward the back of the house, "Matthew, bring those other fellers out front and be careful!"

Soon, four more men in white sheets and those silly pointed hoods rejoined the rest of their kind, prompted by a mighty angry Matthew Green pointing the business end of a Winchester rifle at them.

"Come on, boys, let's go." Whip-holder decided, apparently, his eight-to-one odds still weren't big enough.

They tossed their torches in the dirt, got in their vehicles, and sped away.

"Thank you, Charlie," Pa said as he put the pistol back in his belt. "You got here just in time."

"I'm the one who should be thanking you, Ted. If you hadn't stopped those boys before they beat Matthew they might have killed him. Not many white men would have done that for us."

"I learned in Korea it didn't matter what shade we were on the outside, we all bled red. Anyways, I'm mighty happy to have you as a neighbor. Thank you."

The Despicable Coward

"It's time to rid the world of a despicable coward," Douglas Pennyworth II thought.

The target of Pennyworth's disgust had snuck past a distracted crewman to take the only remaining seat on one of the RMS Titanic's last lifeboats just before it was lowered from the slanting deck of the doomed ship. As the result of his cowardice, the mother and young child to whom that seat would have gone perished in the frigid ocean.

"What a terrible excuse for a man," thought Pennyworth as he tightened the noose around his neck, kicked over the chair beneath his feet, and hung himself.

OOPS!

It was a powder-keg. Tensions between the countries and their allies had grown to the point that almost anything could have been the match that triggered the end of life as we knew it.

Unfortunately, that was me when I lit a brick of firecrackers to impress my friends. I didn't know how near we were to young and inexperienced soldiers on both sides of the border. They heard the explosions, thought they were being attacked, and began firing.

I didn't mean to start a battle that led to a war that would engulf the world.

I turned eighteen today and received my draft call-up. I should have listened to Momma. She always said playing with firecrackers would get me into trouble someday.

Epiphany

Jace Maxwell had never been more miserable.

Only three days ago he'd felt like the luckiest man alive. The company he and his business partner, Harry, had built from scratch was about to be bought for nearly $250 million. Harry recommended they take a cruise to celebrate their success. Nearly halfway through the voyage, they were still celebrating long into the night. At about 3 a.m., Harry suggested they go outside for a breath of fresh air and to take a walk around the deck. At a particularly dark spot, Harry leaned over the railing, pointed and exclaimed, "WOW!" When Jace leaned over to see what his partner was so excited about, Harry pushed him overboard, smiled, and vanished into the shadows.

Jace screamed, but the roar of the engines and the propellers churning the water drowned out his voice. He survived for two terrible days, swimming, then floating to regain some of his strength, then swimming again. Though tormented by terrible thirst and hunger, Jace never gave up. He had a score to settle. Forty-two hours after Harry's betrayal, Jace saw white caps breaking on rocks and swam toward them.

Now, here he was, stuck on what he guessed was an island. While swimming for his life he'd had time to think. Jace kept asking himself why Harry would try to kill him when they both would have been rich. He'd trusted Harry with his life. The answer struck him like a knife in the heart. He and Harry had been so focused on building the company that neither had gotten married. They'd created wills naming the other as their sole beneficiary in the event one of them died. Greed! Harry wanted the entire $250 million for himself!

Jace passed out on the beach, his mind swirling with terrible thoughts.

When dawn broke, Jace explored and found it was an uninhabited island. Miraculously, he discovered a natural spring of fresh water. He wouldn't have to solely rely on capturing rain water, and seafood was plentiful along the island's shores.

He built a lean-to out of palm fronds and, after many hours of trial and error, had started a fire that he never let go completely out. Sixteen days later, he heard a low-flying plane and took a burning stick to light a pile of dead wood he'd been collecting for days to light a signal fire. It was daylight, the fire took too long to light, and no one in the small plane saw it. Jace sunk to his knees in despair.

He didn't stay down for long. Instead of giving up, he experimented with various combinations of combustible items for the signal fire until he had a pile that lit quickly, was bright, and smoked a lot.

The smoke was unnecessary when, on a nearly moonless night about a week later, he heard the drone of another small plane and quickly lit the signal fire. The plane circled, dropped lower, waggled its wings and flew off.

He was rescued the next day. Harry shot himself in the head when he heard the news.

Jace picked up what was left of his life. He'd realized on the island that he'd given up too much of his life focused on merely making money and building a company. He now understood how lonely he'd been while surrounded by people.

He decided it was time to find a life partner and build a family. Jace put as much focus on finding a wife as he did building the company. He didn't want his wealth to attract women who were more attracted to his money than to him so he bought a modest used car, lived in a humble house in a lower-middle-class neighborhood, and never mentioned money when he went on dates.

It took less than a year to find the woman of his dreams. Carol was a girl-next-door type of beauty, with long brown hair that sparkled with tones of red and gold in sunlight, ever-changing deep green eyes that drew him in like the warm waters of the island, an enthusiastic personality, who always looked at the brightest side of things. Most of all, he knew her love for him would last a lifetime.

During that year, he realized how much he missed about living on the island. He often thought of its beauty and tranquility. It even dawned on him one day that the time he'd spent on the island were, in many ways, the happiest he'd ever experienced. Only time spent with Carol matched it in the joy he felt.

Jace and Carol were married on that island. It was the happiest day of their lives.

They named the island Epiphany and often return to it. Each visit brought more joy to them, their children, and grandchildren.

It Had Been So Easy

Benson Hildegard III smiled as he read the news: "Doug Bixby was killed when the barrel of his shotgun exploded while hunting. Investigators determined mud had clogged the barrel and are calling the tragedy an accident. Jasper Johnson, who was with him in the duck blind, narrowly avoided injury."

"Perfect!" Now I'll get the promotion Jasper unfairly gave to Doug just because they were hunting buddies!"

It had been so easy. When Doug got the promotion, Benson pretended to remain his friend and even went to the party Doug threw celebrating the promotion. He'd snuck into Doug's den and found the shotgun that had been laid out for the hunting trip early the next morning. He carefully filled the middle third of its barrel with thick gooey mud he'd taken from the hunting club under cover of darkness the prior evening. He'd kept the thick muck in a plastic bag so it was easy to pour into the barrel, then carefully wiped both ends of the long tube inside and out so a casual observer wouldn't notice anything amiss. Benson figured correctly that Doug wouldn't look down the barrel because the hunter had cleaned it after his trip the prior weekend.

The phone jarred him out of his thoughts. It was Jasper. He was still quite shaken by the accident. Benson played along, "What a terrible tragedy. I'll miss Doug. I'm glad you escaped unhurt." What he was really thinking was, *"Blah, blah, blah. Let's get this over with. Just give me the damned promotion!"*

Sure enough, Jasper gave the promotion to him. While Benson acted surprised and honored, he thought, *"That's better. It's about time!"*

Sitting alone in his apartment, mentally patting himself on the back, Benson looked up and saw his shadow on the wall. He raised his glass of cognac and generously offered a silent toast to his shadow.

He knew at once something wasn't right. Maybe his mind was playing tricks on him. When he raised his glass, his shadow didn't move. It seemed darker than he'd ever seen it, and menacing.

Benson blinked several times, and waved his arms, fully expecting his shadow to mimic his movement as it had done his whole life. Until now. Nothing. No movement at all. *"What the...!"* He closed his eyes, shook his head, and crossed his arms. *"I must be dreaming!"*

Suddenly his shadow spread its arms wide as if reaching for him. Benson jerked back so hard the glass he held shattered against the frame of a bookcase, spraying cognac and shards everywhere. *"I must be going crazy! Got to get out of here!"* He headed for the door, but his shadow reached it first, blocking his path. Benson screamed and tried to run to another room. His silent shadow stayed a step ahead. His screams became shrieks, then screeches. Several neighbors frantically called the police. Benson's voice grew hoarse, and then quieter, until the neighbors thought they heard whimpering.

Officer Knowles began briefing his sergeant as soon as she rushed through the door. "Name's Benson Hildegard III. Dead when I arrived. Body was still warm. All the lights were turned off. He lived alone. No signs of violence. No indication of forced entry. Neighbors heard no one but him. No eyewitnesses."

They looked at what little was left of Benson Hildegard III. He was curled in a fetal position on the floor with his back jammed tightly into a corner. His balled fists clutched a blanket he'd pulled over his head. When they pried the cloth away, it revealed a face frozen in the most horrified look either veteran had ever seen.

Suicide Mission

He awoke from yet another fitful night of sleep. Birds chirped outside his window as the morning's golden filtered light coaxed his reluctant eyes to open. He shook off the fog in his brain and thought about the next few hours. Excitement surged within him mixed with equal parts of anticipation, fear, and resignation. This was it. Today it would happen. He looked at the thick pile of papers on his nightstand, his fingertips resting a moment on them.

After decades of being a successful spy, surviving the most harrowing missions, he was about to embark on a mission from which he wouldn't return. He wouldn't be alone. He and Michelle worked on many missions and saved each other's lives. It was natural they fell in love. It didn't hurt that Michelle was the most beautiful woman he'd ever seen.

They anticipated this assignment for a long time, wondering if this day would ever come.

Tonight she would be in his arms. They would make love–wild, carefree, ravenous, joyous, love. He'd make love like he'd never make love again. He knew it would, indeed, be the last time, but would not speak of it or the reasons for it being so. He'd enjoy the little time they'd have together as they embarked on their final mission together.

He didn't take anything but the clothes on his back. He wouldn't need them.

It wasn't far to the jumping off point, a simple, yet elegant, building of modest size. The lobby was warmly lit with inviting colors. A young woman, Barbara, greeted and showed him to a comfortable chair in a well-lit clean room. She asked if he was ready, and he replied with a confident nod. He received last minute instructions and details. It was critically important to him and to the mission that everything was covered. Mistakes couldn't be tolerated for such an important assignment and there would be no second chances. It was all or nothing and the stakes couldn't be higher. Barbara pushed a button, and the plush chair reclined. She gave him a gentle knowing look, said goodbye, and left.

A team of three walked in, nodding their greetings. He knew them by name. Each had a specialty and they all began to work. No one spoke. One end of a set of long wires was connected to machines, the other end of each had electrodes secured to various parts of his head, over critical parts of his brain. They didn't need to shave his head because precious little hair remained after the rounds of chemo. An IV stand was moved into place beside him and several fluids of various colors were mixed. The doctor named Anne gently took his wrinkled hand and teased a shriveled vein to pop up enough to insert the needle. She whispered, "You'll soon feel no more pain." He smiled broadly. He couldn't remember the last time he'd been without pain; physical pain from the cancer that had spread throughout his body and from the increasingly aggressive things the doctors had done in their attempts to save him, and emotional pain from seeing the woman he loved so dearly losing her battle with an infection that couldn't be stopped and, now, pneumonia.

An orderly wheeled in a bed with the nearly ninety-year-old woman. As he felt the effects of the drugs, he saw a beautiful woman in her prime. Michelle looked at him. With the help of the wires connected to her and the drugs she'd been given, she saw her beloved husband in his prime.

They smiled at each other. He was gently lifted into her bed. They lay on their sides, facing each other, holding hands. Their favorite songs played in the background; lit candles glowed warmly as the lights were lowered. The others left without a word.

Michelle and her beloved husband made love again, for the first time in a long time... and the last time—wild, carefree, ravenous, joyous, love. They agreed it was the best they ever had. All the touching was in their minds and hearts.

Then, the hearts that had beat together for a lifetime, joyfully beat once more and stopped.

Without a Hitch

"The heist went off without a hitch," thought Victor. Six million bucks worth of high-quality un-cut diamonds. They ditched the stolen getaway car in a crowded parking lot near where Victor's car was parked. The three men were careful to pick a lot that was out of the view of security cameras.

Victor drove his two partners in his car deep into the woods. George and Hank's vehicles were miles away in different directions and parked among several other vehicles near trail heads. Victor parked and began walking toward a large stump forty feet away. "Let's divide the stones over here. Get them." As Hank turned toward the car, George hesitated just long enough to see and return Victor's nod.

Victor reached the stump, watched, and waited for his plan to play out, thinking, *"It'll soon all be mine!"*

Hank opened the trunk lid and leaned inside. George pulled his gun. BANG! Hank arched his back and crumpled. The acrid smoke of gunpowder tickled George's nose. He grabbed the treasure and walked past Victor to lay the containers on the stump.

Victor turned, pulled his gun and called George's name. George turned and took a step back when he saw the gun pointed at him. "No! Wait! You promised..."

"You fool!" Victor gloated. "Did you really think I'd share any of this with you?" He took his time, savoring the moment, slowly moving the barrel of his gun to the center of George's chest. BANG!

But, it was Victor who slumped to the ground and died moments later with a bewildered look on his face.

Hank walked up to George and said with a smile: "I'm sure glad your gun was firing blanks."

"I'm sure glad yours wasn't. When Victor plotted to have me kill you, I knew neither of us would be safe while he was alive. Thanks for playing along."

Hank looked down at the bloody corpse. "Too bad he got greedy. There was plenty for all of us."

Hard Bargain

The food supply on Nopporg was nearly exhausted. Nopporgians would begin starving in a year or two if new food sources from other planets weren't quickly found. Earth was the nearest planet that had similar growing conditions, and food was plentiful in large parts of it.

Nopporgians were technically superior to Earthlings and could have taken the food by force but chose to negotiate. The Earthlings, sensing a desperate buyer, drove a hard bargain, but an agreement was reached.

The latter's huge ship was filled with over a thousand head of cattle, plus many other farm animals, and seeds for over one hundred types of fruits and vegetables. Additionally, over three hundred people joined the great adventure to help Earth's neighbors save themselves. Ranchers and farmers, specialists from a wide variety of disciplines, including sustainable farming and ranching, irrigation, water preservation, and animal husbandry were excited about the opportunity to share their knowledge and skill. Their families were allowed to join them. Many more would-be adventurers were turned away for lack of capacity.

As the great ship blasted off, second-in-command, Leejed, smiled. "We have everything we need, and the Earthlings appear thrilled."

His leader, Tresong, nodded. "Yes. I don't think they'd be nearly so excited if they knew that after they teach us how to grow their food, we're going to eat them, too."

Crescendo

My hand trembles when I touch her cheek. I feel the warmth of her breath on my fingertip as I trace her lips, drawn by the irresistible outline of her mouth. She reacts with an uncontrolled quiver, then tentatively begins to draw my finger into her mouth with the slightest movement of her lips. Her tongue teases, promising ever-greater pleasure, drawing me deeper inside.

Capturing just a finger, my temptress enslaves all of me. I inhale sharply. Even my breath is at the mercy of her magic.

Leaning down, I nibble an earlobe and am rewarded by a gasp of delight and another quiver. My tongue begins there, exploring every curve and crease of her enchanting ear.

Our touches conquer mysterious unexplored lands, promising and delivering great treasures.

Every exhale from me draws an inhale from her as our hearts beat in sync, a symphony of passion building, building.

With every motion, every touch, the ecstatic tension grows. Our bodies beg to make it last forever, putting off as long as possible a crescendo we sense is coming that threatens to drown our bodies and minds with overwhelming wave after wave of pleasure.

Hours later, we're awakened by the golden glow of sunrise and the gentle touch of a cool breeze. We stretch. Our eyes meet. The joy and gratitude we see reflected in them puts beaming smiles on our faces and leads to a lingering good morning kiss that promises many more to come.

We pull ourselves into our wheelchairs to begin the day.

Inseparable

Mary and Hope were lifelong best friends, and Jason and Ted had an unbreakable bond of camaraderie. The moment the men saw the ladies at a county fair, it was love at first sight. It was the same for Mary and Hope. In their early twenties, their happiness grew without bounds.

The two couples did everything together. Exactly one year later, Mary and Jason got married on the same day as Hope and Ted.

They even shared the same bed on their honeymoons. The brides were conjoined twins, as were their husbands.

Saddle Buddies

Sam and Joe met in Saint Louis when they were both on their way to gold country. Sam was headed west to help a brother build a ranch on land they'd just bought, and Joe was off to seek his fortune. They became fast friends.

The trip was as long and arduous as they'd heard. Two thousand miles of hardship and danger: Indian attacks, snakes (human and reptilian), sleeping in the rain, fording swollen rivers, slogging through mud and early snowstorms, and running low on water and food. Through every challenge they had each other's back and saved each other more times than they could count.

When, at last, they reached San Francisco, they got married.

Joe Johnston had found his treasure long before reaching the rowdy young gold town, and Samantha "Sam" Burdock had known from the start she'd found a man worth fighting for.

The Fog

Melissa was drawn to the hill from the moment she inherited this property from an aunt she'd never met. It was always shrouded in fog. The fog remained through rainstorms and when everywhere else was sunny.

Melissa was a quadriplegic from a childhood accident. Her wheelchair was battery-powered but couldn't climb the hill. One day, she hired me to push her to the summit. With her cat, Curiosity, in her lap, I moved them up the long slope. After much effort, we reached the fog line.

I sat to catch my breath, and Curiosity stretched her way off Melissa's lap to investigate the new surroundings. Melissa motored toward the fog, first with hesitant movements, then with growing confidence. She disappeared when the fog enveloped her.

A moment later, she walked out of the fog. I thought I was hallucinating. Walked!?

She wore the most amazing smile and a beautiful dress of a shimmering material that reflected the sunlight. Melissa looked about ten years older, but the laugh lines looked good on her.

I sat in shock when Melissa picked up Curiosity. She looked at me with radiant, twinkling eyes, put a finger to her lips, winked, and nodded toward the fog. Without a word, she returned to it.

It was the last anyone here ever saw of her, or of me.

Fog of War

The war dragged on for years, becoming a stalemate. Everyone hoped it might lead to a truce, and, perhaps, elusive peace.

When a fog appeared out of nowhere on a sunny day, Sgt. Joe Turner, had just enough time to yell "Poison Gas! Put on your gear" before it enveloped him.

He came to a moment later and could see fifty times further and hear a twig snap or smell a cigarette burning a mile away. When he focused on the enemy, he seemed to have a sixth sense about what their leaders were thinking.

These attributes came in handy on the battlefield. It was as if the fog of war had been permanently lifted from his mind. His squad began winning every battle. He got promoted again and again and soon commanded whole armies. The tide of war turned strongly in their favor. It wouldn't be long before they would demand unconditional surrender.

Without warning, 5-Star General Joe Turner collapsed into a coma. At the same moment, behind the enemy lines, a fog suddenly appeared and enveloped Unteroffizier Hans Schmidt.

Three months later, Forward Observer Ryrtle reported to his home planet. "It's working! These foolish Earthlings are doing all our work for us. We'll soon be able to take their planet without firing a shot!"

A Fairy Tale for Grown-Up Children

There once was a young man who lived in a big old city. One day, he fell in love with a beautiful woman. He learned too late that she had an ugly heart. She treated him very unkindly and then left him, breaking his heart. Because he'd been treated so badly, the young man began treating everyone the same way.

Most people didn't like being treated that way and left his life. The ones who stayed treated him as badly as he treated them and he became miserable.

It seemed that people only brought pain, so he decided to go as far away from people as he could; he went deep into the forest and built a cabin.

At first, he was very lonely, but, at least, he wasn't being hurt anymore. He studied the animals and plants of the forest and noticed how they often worked together. Squirrels buried nuts so other squirrels could find them and none would starve in the winter. Birds or other animals who sensed danger raised alarms that all animals could hear so all kinds of animals would be safer. Trees protected many animals and provided them with homes and shade. None waited to be treated well by the others before taking care of them.

The young man learned much from the forest and became friends with the many living things that shared it with him. He was happy, but he was lonely for a mate. Night after night he asked the stars to bring a young woman to him, and, night after night, he fell asleep alone.

Then, one day he heard a woman crying for help. He ran through the forest and found a beautiful woman, sobbing. One look, and he fell in love with her.

"Hello. My name is Andrew. May I help you?"

The woman stopped sobbing and said, "I'm Lucinda and I'm lost. I was picking berries but saw a bear and got scared and ran and ran. Now, I don't know where I am."

"You're in the middle of the forest. You must be hungry. He reached into a pouch that was tied to his belt and offered some food to her. She liked being taken care of and decided to stay with him. That made him happy, but it didn't take long for the ugliness in Lucinda's heart to show. No matter how hard Andrew tried to please her, she complained and wanted more. She never helped with anything. He was miserable again. To his surprise, he felt lonely despite living with someone.

Even his animal friends avoided her.

It seemed he hadn't yet learned some lessons well enough.

One day, when Lucinda was away from the cabin washing in a nearby creek, another woman came into the clearing where Andrew had built his cabin. "Hello, I'm Lori. My sister got lost in the forest, and I'm trying to find her."

"Hi, I'm Andrew. Your sister has been staying here. She'll be back shortly. You must be hungry. Would you like some food? He reached into a pouch on his belt and, as he handed some food to her, he noticed she had kind eyes and a friendly smile. She noticed the same thing about him and the first seeds of love took root in their hearts. The animals came out to welcome her.

Lucinda walked up and the animals scattered. She saw Lori and snarled, "Oh, it's you. What are you doing here?"

"Dear sister, I went looking for you when you didn't come back from picking berries. I thought you might be lost and in danger."

"I'm not lost and the only danger I'm in is of being bored to death. I'm sick of this place, and sick of HIM," she scowled, pointing to Andrew.

"I tied red ribbons on my trail into the forest," Lori said. "If you are so miserable and want to leave you'll be able to find your way out."

"Good! Are you coming with me?"

Andrew's heart skipped a beat, and he blurted to Lori, "You're welcome to stay here if you like."

"I think I'd like that, at least for a while."

Andrew provided food for Lucinda's journey and wished her well. The sisters hugged goodbye and Lucinda left.

Andrew and Lori didn't live happily ever after. As in all lives, there were times of sadness and illness, but their joy greatly outweighed their sadness. And, they never took for granted all the blessings they shared.

Piggyback

Lt. Paul Dawson was miserable. *"This whole mission has been one nightmare after another. Our communications systems with Earth stopped working as soon as we hit this planet's atmosphere. I'd just started the thermal scan when that arrogant idiot captain, the insufferable whiner ordered me to explore the planet's surface with him before all the planet's readings were conducted. Foolish and totally against protocol. He probably needs to have someone hold his hand..."*

"Hurry up, Lieutenant!" Dawson heard over his intercom.

"Yes, sir!"

The captain was about seventy paces ahead.

Back on the crew-less ship, the thermal scanner picked up something and forwarded it to Dawson's reader. It beeped. His pace slowed as he looked at the readings. "What the...? He saw beings that were invisible to the naked eye, but with infrared, their heat signatures gave them away. They appeared to be nearly square, only about three feet tall and covered in tiny appendages. "Odd looking."

"Maybe they're harmless and just trying to hide from us. I see no weapons. Just in case..."

"Uh, Captain. You might want to see this."

The captain, engrossed in viewing the purple-tinted terrain, ignored him.

Touched

Suddenly, the beings on the scanner appeared to multiply at will as they moved in front of the Captain. They piled on top of each other like a human pyramid that reminded Dawson of kids' building blocks. "Captain, LOOK OUT!"

The captain heard the warning just as the wall of sentient building blocks reached fifteen feet high and nine feet wide, then dropped and crushed him. The captain's pressure suit imploded and then exploded.

"CAPTAIN!" Dawson turned. *"Gotta get back to Earth. Warn them!"* He ran toward the ship and ordered, "LOWER RAMP!" The ship obeyed. He ran in and shut the door before anything chasing him could reach it.

He never saw the two stowaways who waited near the ship for the terrified Earthling to let them in ahead of him.

Irony

It was a historic day for Earthlings and Resividans alike. First contact had been made on the latter's planet and both sides wanted peace. Per ancient tradition, the leader of the Resividan delegation poured sacred water into the Peace Cup, and everyone drank from it. After the ceremony was complete, the Earthlings headed for home.

Unfortunately, germs each side naturally carried that were harmless on their home planet were deadly to those from the other planet. Within two weeks, everyone who drank from the Peace Cup was dead.

Both sides suspected the other of treachery and assassination via poison. Deciding diplomacy had failed, they then relied on something that had been an ancient tradition on both their planets.

War.

Coming Out Party

Bobby Joe McCoy knew he was different than most and always would be. There was no denying it, but in so many important ways, he was just like everyone else. He loved and needed to be loved; wanted to be of use, valued, and respected; craved to be touched, hugged, and to feel connected and accepted.

He built up his courage, knowing there would be stares, whispers behind his back, and ignorant hurtful things said to his face.

His friends urged him to come out when he was ready. They were there for him now, waiting outside in the pleasant warmth of the spring sun, not the cold artificial light he'd been in for so long. Bobby Joe craved to feel the warmth of the sun again.

He knew in his heart that he couldn't, *wouldn't* wait a moment longer. He took a deep breath, rolled through the doors of the army's burn clinic and down the ramp and into the arms of his friends and family. With much of his body and face no longer recognizable to him, Sergeant Bobby Joe McCoy was finally ready to begin the next chapter of his life.

The sun felt wonderful, but not nearly as good as being surrounded by family and friends. He knew that, with their love and support, somehow he'd make it.

Interstellar Invitation

They lived among us for days and we had no clue. That changed on a warm summer night.

Michelle and I were enjoying the tantalizing scent and sound of popping kettle corn at a charity carnival when fireworks suddenly burst high over our town square. They were so bright they almost hurt our eyes, and the images they depicted were far more elaborate than we'd ever seen.

One set showed a puppy jumping through hoops. Then a train raced across the sky, into a tunnel, and emerged with dozens of colors exploding from its smokestack. The spectacular grand finale was a spaceship that shot across the sky and appeared as if it were about to land at the end of Main Street in a finale of bright bursts and colors.

As the smoke cleared, we were astonished to see the spaceship wasn't just a fireworks display. It was real and glowed with the colors of a rainbow, pulsing in a soothing rhythm. A soft gust of wind touched our faces as it silently settled onto the street.

We gasped in surprise at the apparition in front of us. It towered at least four stories high, was about forty feet wide, and, perhaps, fifty feet long.

Several people emerged from the crowd and stood in front of the mysterious hulking thing, facing us. We'd seen them around town during the prior few days and assumed they worked for the carnival company or, perhaps, were traveling salespeople. We don't get many strangers in our secluded town because it is far from a major highway.

The tallest of the strangers, a man with a big smile and friendly face spoke in a relaxed tone that had a calming effect. "Please, don't be alarmed. We're from this spacecraft. We've come from a distant star and are on a journey of exploration. This is the first time we've visited your planet and decided to stop and spend a few of your earth days here. We've enjoyed our visit. You have been nice to us and we would like to return the favor.

"About three of your earth years ago, we began a journey to explore many other planetary systems before we go home about seven or eight years from now. We would be happy to take some of you with us. We'll be passing near your planet again on our way home and could return you here on our return trip. We have all you will need on board, including ample breathable air, water, and food. We'll give a tour of our ship to anyone who is seriously interested in accepting our invitation.

Michelle grabbed my hand and we were first in line in front of a ramp that ascended to a large opening that appeared like magic in the smooth skin of the ship.

Michelle and I had been married for twenty-seven years. Our only child died as an infant and we were too heartbroken to have another. We loved our town, yet had often talked of going on a great adventure for an extended vacation. Michelle always dreamed of going into space and, for the first time in her life, a chance to do so dropped out of the sky at our feet. She wasn't about to miss this great opportunity.

I was open to the idea but had a lot of concerns and, reluctantly, tagged along as we climbed the ramp and entered the ship.

The interior had many gentle curves and was soft and warm to the touch. Each chamber was well-lit with warm glowing lights that appeared wherever we went throughout the ship and gradually faded as we moved away from them into other chambers.

The tall man who had greeted us in the square introduced himself as Olox Captain. He explained his surname reflected his position or role much like how some of the surnames on our planet had been created from roles, such as Smith or Porter.

"We have a small crew and ample room for up to twenty human guests. You're probably wondering why we would invite beings that are alien to us on our journey. The answer, quite simply, is because we can and because we find it pleasurable to share our experiences with others, much as you do when you invite someone to enjoy a sunset with you."

The air inside the vessel tasted clean and fresh. Our guides demonstrated the synthesizers for creating food, water, air, medicines, and clothes and showed us how easy they were to operate. Each guest would have a small but comfortable space for sleeping and privacy.

Our hosts invited us to sit in comfortable chairs. When we did, the chairs slowly and gently began to tilt backward so we faced toward a large domed ceiling. On it appeared many dazzling and enchanting images. "These are some of the worlds, moons, systems, and galaxies we plan to explore," Olox Captain explained. The phrase "Breathtaking and awe-inspiring" doesn't begin to express the magnificence of the images we experienced.

We, the guests, asked many questions and received answers that appeared to delight quite a few of us.

When the show ended, Olox Captain said, "As I mentioned before, we can only take up to twenty of you. Since you are the first twenty to visit us, you will have the first chance to accept our invitation. Either way, we must leave within an hour. We wish we could give you more time, but we don't want to have to deal with authorities on your planet who might not take kindly to our visit or who might attempt to keep us here against our wishes. We've temporarily blocked all communications to and from your town but it is possible someone may have seen us land and plans to inform the authorities. We plan to be gone before they arrive.

"If you want to come with us, you'll barely have time to write a note to your loved ones and to gather a few small belongings. We can accommodate one large bag per person.

"Please, go now and briefly talk it over. Let us know in the next thirty minutes if you commit to joining us. Remember, we take off in an hour and won't wait for anyone. Please don't be late."

I'd watched Michelle's growing enthusiasm throughout the tour. When we were off the ship, she bubbled with excitement and sounded almost giddy as she said, "I had some concerns, but they addressed each one. I'll miss our families and friends, but this opportunity is *way* too good to pass up, and of course, we'll be sharing this great adventure together!"

She looked to see my reaction. "Wait, what's wrong? You look sick."

"I can't go."

It was as if I'd pricked her inflated balloon. "Why not?" she asked. Her expression seemed to be a combination of shock and pain.

"I'd love to go, but there are too many small places on the ship that triggered my claustrophobia. I don't talk about it much because I'm embarrassed by it, but that's why I've always resisted going on cruises."

"Well, if you're not going, I'm not going."

"You've *got* to go! How many times have I heard you say how much you loved going to Space Camp as a kid? You've dreamed of being an astronaut your whole life! Here's your chance to explore the universe! How often does such an opportunity like this come up? NEVER!"

Tears fell down her cheeks. She wiped them away with her hand and shook her head from side-to-side, then turned without saying a word and raced to the ship. I followed her up the ramp.

Olox Captain greeted us, a concerned look on his face. "Have we done something to offend you?"

"Not at all," Michelle replied, wiping more tears away. You have been wonderful, and your invitation is most generous. We'd love to go with you but can't."

"May I ask why?"

"Because, well uh, it's kind of personal. I..." Michelle looked down. She was trying to avoid embarrassing me.

"It's because I'm claustrophobic," I blurted.

"Ah yes. That's the fear of confined spaces, if I'm not mistaken."

"Yes. I have a fairly extreme case of it."

"I can see why that would seem to be an insurmountable problem for you to be on such a small ship. Would you please come with me? I'd like to show you something."

I nodded. We followed him back inside the vessel, walked a bit and came to a small chamber that appeared designed as a sleeping and privacy area for one person. "Would being in there make you uncomfortable?"

"Yes."

Olox touched the frame of the doorway and said, "Enlarge by one-half." He removed his hand from the frame and within seconds the room grew fifty percent larger. He turned to me and asked, "How about now?"

Our mouths dropped. Michelle caught herself first, closed her mouth, put a finger beneath my chin, and gently pushed upward as she winked and smiled at me.

Speechless, I walked into the much-enlarged room. The space was now plenty big enough that it didn't trigger my claustrophobia. I smiled and nodded. "This would work."

Olox offered, "We can make this or any room or combination of rooms on the ship many times larger or smaller as the need or convenience calls for it."

"B-but how?" Michelle stammered.

"Our ship is made out of hyper-flexible materials that can expand and contract. The floor space of rooms that aren't being used can be reduced to a very small fraction of their in-use size. This allows us to optimize the size of each room to what is needed at that moment. We can even change the outer dimensions of our ship, but don't often do that because it takes a lot of energy to transform the whole ship in that way."

I was barely listening, still focused on what he'd just done to the room. "But what happens when people are occupying a space and someone else needs to enlarge or shrink it? Seems like that would be jarring, or at least disorienting to those inside."

"When there are occupants, rooms resize much more slowly than when they are empty. If needed, equipment and furniture within the room can also adjust in size when practical to assist in the transformation and to minimize disorientation for existing occupants. You'll be surprised as to how quickly you'll adjust.

"Every room and space already recognizes each of your voices. Once you find an optimal size for each chamber, you can set it as your dimensions by adding the word "default" to the brief sizing request you make when you touch a doorframe. Rooms can never become so small as to trap or hurt occupants, and each occupant is automatically given whatever minimum personal space they need to feel comfortable.

"Everything in each space, including furniture, equipment, shelving, and facilities, also automatically adjusts to be optimally useful and comfortable for those who are substantially shorter or taller than average. Even ceilings adjust.

Olox beamed and I thought he looked like an excited little boy showing off his shiny new toys. He said, "Please come this way. I want to show you something else!"

He took us the food synthesizers, turned toward us and paused. "I'm sorry; I don't even know your names."

"I'm James Carson and this is my wife, Michelle."

"Nice to meet you both. I'd now like to demonstrate our food synthesizers. James, please tell this unit what you'd like to eat it right now. Don't hold back. Be as challenging as possible."

I thought for a moment, smiled mischievously, and said, "I'd like a one-inch-thick bison steak cooked medium rare, lightly covered in blackberry sauce."

"That may take a few moments," Olox said.

By the time he finished the sentence, a panel opened and a sizzling bison steak appeared, exactly as I'd requested. Its aroma was exquisite. Olox reached into a bin and brought out a knife and fork. "Please, enjoy it while it's hot."

I sliced off a large chunk and plunged it into my mouth. An explosion of flavor lit up my taste buds. I closed my eyes, savoring every burst and nuance. My grin must have been ear-to-ear.

"What would you like to try, Michelle?" he asked.

"Oh, no, thank you! I'm much too excited to eat!"

"Well, then, I only have one more question to ask you: Do you accept our invitation to join us on our journey?

Enthusiastic nods gave our answer to him before he'd finished his question, then we quickly excused ourselves to go pack and say our goodbyes.

The End. Or, perhaps, it's just the beginning...

Bonus Material

Here are my stories which were included in ***Palpable Imaginings,*** an anthology of fiction short stories from selected writers. They're followed by a couple of stories which may become the initial chapters in a novel or novella I'm considering writing.

I Only Wanted to Be Their Friend

"I only wanted to be their friend," Chris thought to himself.

He joined the popular boys' organization after his family moved away from his other school and friends. He craved friendship and companionship but often experienced ridicule and pain.

He was told on his first camping trip to beware the dreaded Black Booger Disease. When one is camping, dust and dirt often turn the inside of one's nose a dark brown or black, but new campers may not be aware of it and can be frightened by the threat of having the imaginary Black Booger Disease when they noticed their snot getting darker.

Then there was the Snipe Hunt where everyone went out at night with burlap sacks to catch the elusive but "very tasty" birds. The older boys set Chris and the other new kids in position in the dark woods by themselves and said they'll drive any Snipes toward them by making noise, but instead went back to camp, leaving the new boys standing in the dark holding bags for a bird that was nowhere to be found.

At events with hundreds of participants, older boys sent Chris and other new members to the far end of the campground to ask other units if they could borrow a Left-Handed Smoke Shifter. Of course, there is no such thing as a Left-Handed Smoke-Shifter, so when asked, the older boys at the far end of the camp "helpfully" suggested that they heard there was one at another far corner of the camp.

Once, when the backpacks of the younger boys were inspected to ensure they were packed properly, a couple of the oldest boys, Vincent and Martin, sent Chris off to do an errand. While he was away, they took all the heaviest items from the other backpacks and put them into Chris's. When everyone went for a hike up a steep trail, Chris could barely climb it while the older boys breezed past, taunting him. Two of the younger boys, Ron and Jack, stayed with Chris, and even helped him carry the extra weight.

The adult leaders could be cruel as well. Once, when a stranger's car got stuck in mud and he honked an SOS. The boys wanted to go with the leader in his car to help, but there wasn't enough room for everyone. The leader looked Chris up and down, sneered, and said, "You're too skinny. Stay here."

The cruelest cut came when the boys were camping on Chris's birthday. Vincent and Martin baked a small cake for him. Thinking he had finally passed their "tests" for acceptance, Chris was thrilled with their gift and symbol of friendship.

Shortly afterward, Chris was stricken with a severe case of diarrhea. It kept him incapacitated for the whole weekend. Vincent bragged they'd put dish soap in the cake mix. Ron and Jack brought water to Chris and tried to keep his spirits up after the infamous birthday cake trick.

During the camping trip the following month, at Chris' suggestion, Ron and Jack wore long sleeve shirts and gloves as they helped him gather wood. When they arrived at the campsite with loaded arms, Vincent, Martin, and the other older boys took it from them.

"Thanks for the firewood!" Vincent gloated.

As usual, Chris said nothing. He stared sadly at Ron and Jack, then pulled out a large clear bag of home-made gorp and offered it to his two new friends. Vincent grabbed the bag of mixed nuts, granola, dried fruit, and large bits of chocolate. He walked away, yelling to the older boys, "Look what Chris brought for us."

Vincent and his buddies gobbled down big handfuls; then built a roaring fire and began whittling and practicing their lashings with the wood Chris and his new friends had collected.

The three youngest boys chose to play cards well away from the smoky fire and out of earshot of the others.

Smiling, Ron said, "They're going to be sorry they stole all that wood with poison oak from us."

Jack chuckled, looked at Chris, and added, "I can't wait for those chocolate laxative pieces in the gorp to hit 'em."

Chris smiled, then added with sad eyes, "I only wanted to be their friend."

Tough Night at the Lumber Mill

I was bored and sleepy. The night was not what I expected. Earlier that day, my grandfather asked me if I wanted to go to work with him. He was the graveyard shift night watchman at a lumber mill near Murphy Creek, Oregon. I didn't know what a graveyard shift was or what a night watchman did, but it sounded exciting and a little scary so I said, "Sure!"

I was a scrawny nine-year-old California city kid visiting my grandparents in the country. I felt honored to go to work with him. As the oldest of five children, I believed that being invited could start a traditional rite of passage for all my siblings. It turns out, I was the first *and last* to be invited because of what happened that night.

The hours ticked by. It was dark by the time Grandma made dinner for us to take to work and a thermos of coffee for him. Watching Grandpa get ready, I was disappointed that he wore regular clothes. I expected him to have a uniform and badge.

Then, he strapped on a holster and gun. *"Oh boy! He needs a gun to do his job! Cool! This is going to be great! He must really trust me to invite me to a dangerous job where he needs to use a gun!"*

I yelled "Shotgun" to myself as I sat in the front seat next to him in his old pickup. I was his sidekick, ready to back him up if things got rough. Maybe we'd even catch some robbers or something.

The workers had gone home. We were all alone to protect this huge mysterious lumber mill. A howling wind chilled my bones, sent shivers up my spine, and quickly blew away puffy clouds of mist that appeared when we spoke. The whole place smelled like sawdust and freshly-cut wood. The night was cloudy and as black as our cat Tiffany. I missed her. A full moon added flickering light when fast-moving clouds thinned out in places, a potent mix of magic and spookiness.

We went into the guard shack. Grandpa rarely said much. I learned from my dad that men who say little are often the ones you want to listen to the most. They think a lot before saying anything. Unlike me; I often chatter nervously. It was almost as if I were afraid of the silence. My incessant talking must have driven my grandpa nuts, but he never mentioned it.

We sat together in the guard shack trying to keep warm. After what seemed like hours, he said it was time to do our rounds. I didn't know what he meant, but I followed him out the door. On the way out, he grabbed the strap of something black and hung it from his shoulder. Whenever a beam of light fell on it, I stole a glance at it trying to figure out what it was. The mysterious item was the shape of a thick solid wheel made of metal encased in leather. It had what looked like a small clock in the center and something that looked like a big keyhole.

As we walked around the lumber mill, few bright lights pierced small holes in the darkness. I guessed those were the most important places for us to protect. In the full-dark places, Grandpa used a flashlight to keep us from crashing into things. Occasionally, Grandpa stopped to lift a metal lid from a small box that held a key on a chain. He inserted and twisted the key into the mysterious round leather-encased object, then put the key back where he found it. Near as I could tell, the key never opened anything. I asked him what he was doing. He said it was how he showed that he was doing his rounds when and where he was supposed to. It seemed like magic to me.

Walking around empty buildings and in the dark was scary, but I had my grandpa with me and he had his gun. Besides, we were doing an important job. No telling when someone might try to rob the place.

When our rounds were done, we went back to the guard shack. He offered some coffee to me. *"Wow! Adults drink coffee and he just offered me some. He must think I'm grownup enough to handle it."* I proudly accepted a cup. It was bitter compared to hot chocolate, but it was hot. I'd have finished it even if it tasted like mud. I didn't want him thinking his grandson was a wimp.

I got bored. Then drowsy. The hours dragged on in the guard shack. I wished something exciting would hurry up and happen. I didn't want to waste the night. I tried real hard to stay awake, trying not to wimp out; and sidekicks need to stay awake when on duty. I fell asleep.

I don't know how long I was out. The next thing I knew, Grandpa was shaking my arm. I jerked my head off the table. It took me a second to get my eyes to focus and realize where I was.

He whispered, "I hear something out there. Stay here. I'll be back shortly." He grabbed his flashlight and was gone.

I felt excited, then scared. *"What if something bad happens to Grandpa? He might need my help."* I didn't want to admit even to myself that I was afraid of being in that guard shack alone, in a big saw mill, in the middle of the night, in the middle of nowhere. I wanted to be with him. I quietly slipped out the door. I didn't have a flashlight and couldn't see a thing. I was even more afraid.

I considered going back in the guard house. Conflicting thoughts and feelings battled in my brain. *"What if Grandpa needs me? What can I do? I'm just a kid! He told me to stay in the shack. It's scarier out here than in there. But, I'm closer to Grandpa out here."* I like to think the question "What if Grandpa needs me?" was the only reason I didn't go back. However, I'm sure the "I'm closer to Grandpa out here" was the more appealing part of my thinking.

"Which way did he go?"

I heard what sounded like loud voices and stumbled in the darkness toward the sounds.

As I got closer, flickering moonlight from a partial break in the clouds created an eerie scene of three angry young men standing in front of Grandpa. I hid behind the corner of a building about twenty feet away. I noticed how old grandpa looked. The lenses in his glasses were as thick as the bottoms of soda bottles. He was never very tall and was now stooped with age. He wheezed from bad lungs as the result of smoking and working in a bakery and saw mill all his life.

I heard Grandpa say, "Boys, you are trespassing and need to leave."

The biggest one, who stood at least six inches taller than Grandpa, was probably forty pounds heavier, and fifty years younger, looked at his buddies and laughed, sneering, "Go away old man. Our party is just getting started." He lifted a can of beer and chugged it.

Grandpa sighed, and said bit louder, "Go. NOW!"

The man in the middle took two steps forward and stared in Grandpa's face, then spit on the ground near Grandpa's boots. "Who's going to make me, OLD man?" He pushed Grandpa. Just then, clouds completely covered the moon, and I couldn't see a thing.

In the darkness, a big bang like a sledge hammer hitting a piece of wooden post hung in the air. When moonlight filtered through like a strobe-light, I only saw three men standing. I panicked until I noticed Grandpa was one of them. In the flickering light, I saw the loud-mouthed thug on the ground writhing in pain and holding a nose spurting blood.

His buddies crouched and were ready to pounce. Grandpa rested his palm on the pistol in his holster and calmly said, "I've asked you twice to leave. I won't ask again."

Whether it was Grandpa's comment, quick reflexes, or gun—perhaps all three—but, it took the starch out of them. They picked up their writhing ringleader, got in their hot rod, and left in a flickering cloud of dust.

Grandpa saw and walked over to me. I thought I was going to get a lecture about being told to stay in the guard shack. Instead, grandpa just had a wily grin on his face as he said, "They didn't know I used to be a boxer. C'mon, let's finish our rounds."

Terror on Interstate 5

What started as an exciting adventure turned into the most terrifying time of my life. It happened in the early '70s in the middle of the night on a long and lonely stretch of Interstate 5 between distant small farming communities.

My mom and her friend, Mary, were taking their children to Disneyland. Mary was driving late at night so the smaller kids would sleep during most of the 400-mile trip. All seven of us were jammed into our Travel-All, a large SUV-type vehicle with huge, heavy tires made for four-wheeling.

At age fifteen, I was the oldest of the kids and got to sit with the adults on the less-crowded front bench seat. It was warm and quiet, and I was excited about Disneyland but already missing a girl at school.

BLAM-BANG! Our vehicle began wobbling wildly as if the big beast was trying to decide whether to flip over sideways or end-over-end. We started spinning while bucking from side to side. A kaleidoscope of zigzagging spinning lights streaked all around us as we grabbed for something to hang onto in sheer terror. We braced for the inevitable crash or roll.

Time seemed to slow to a crawl while our world spun out of control in a fast-motion nightmare. When we finally stopped spinning, we were hit with a shockwave of the blaring horns and glaring lights of two rapidly approaching eighteen-wheelers. Our dazed brains realized that we were straddling both lanes facing the wrong way on the freeway.

With no time to react, we watched in sheer terror as the big rigs roared past, inches from each side, violently rocking our rig. We were all shaking even after our vehicle stopped moving.

Mary drove the stricken Travel-All to the side of the freeway. After making sure the kids were not hurt other than bumped noggins and knees, Mom told them to stay in the rig. She, Mary, and I got out to see what happened.

The stench of burned rubber hung in the air. In the intermittent light of passing cars, we saw that both a front and rear tire diagonally opposite each other had blown. We were lucky to be alive. But, we remained in a dangerous situation, stuck on the side of the freeway with one spare tire and two flats, on a dark night with traffic whizzing past.

A big rig stopped and two men got out. They checked our spare tire then jacked up the Travel-All to replace one of the damaged tires. They took off the second tire and offered to take one of us to the nearest town where they knew someone who worked in a garage and could help us.

I didn't want either my mom or Mary to be alone with two strange men on a dark highway, and I knew they didn't want to leave their little ones. As the oldest kid, it was up to me to go. I was scared, but going with them seemed the best of several bad options.

The men smiled and seemed friendly enough so my mom reluctantly agreed to let me go with the men for help. She gave me some money to pay the garage guy.

The men put the ruined tire in a spare tire rack under their trailer. They said the garage guy would fix the tire and then come back with me to put on the fixed tire.

I saw the worried looks on Mom's and Mary's faces as one of the men said in a friendly voice, "C'mon, son, climb in." I grabbed my jacket, waved goodbye to my mom and climbed into the cab.

It was dark inside. At the time, I didn't think to wonder why the truck's dome light didn't come on when the doors were opened. The driver told me to sit in the back. As I turned to do as he said, my right hand touched the top of the driver's seatback and felt something semi-liquid and sticky. I pulled my hand away and wiped it on my pants. It was too dark to see.

I'd never been in the cab of a big rig before. Behind the front seats was an area with what felt like a bed nearly the width of the cab. I guessed it must be where truckers slept when they were on long hauls far from home. The men didn't say anything as the driver pulled onto the highway. I was surprised by the loud noise of the engine and noticed the extra gear shifts it took to get up to highway speed.

I sat on the edge of the bed hoping the trip to the garage would be short. After a few miles, we passed a lighted exit, a glowing oasis in a desert of darkness. As we drove past, the light lit their faces for a moment just as the men turned to glance at each other. The cold looks on their faces drove a big chill up my spine.

I asked how much further until we got to the garage. Neither answered, but the one who wasn't driving turned toward me. In the darkness, I didn't see his left arm as he swung it around and back-handed me across my face. The blow was lightning fast, and, like lightning, I saw a flash as it flung me across the bed. My head spun. My lips were bleeding. He growled, "Shut up kid! Say another word and I'll kill you."

That's when I noticed my head hadn't hit the bed. I thought I'd banged it into the wall behind the bed, but, as my eyes and mind tried to refocus, I realized it was softer than a wall, harder than a bed, and about nine inches above the bed's surface.

I felt behind me in the darkness. Whatever it was, moved! I jerked my hand away. The movement had been very slight, but it petrified me. I heard a muffled moan. Again, ever so slight. At first, I thought I'd imagined it. Twisting around and feeling, I realized it was a prone adult.

Moving my shaking hands in the darkness toward what I hoped was the person's head, I felt a neck, then a chin. When I reached the area where I thought his mouth would be, instead of feeling lips, I touched something flat. The mouth area was covered in the same semi-liquid sticky substance I'd felt on the top of the driver's seat.

My mind raced. Blood! It's gotta be blood! The mouth was covered with some kind of tape. Probably duct tape. Scared beyond sanity, I turned to face the front.

When we passed under a highway sign light, I attempted to learn as much as I could about the men and their faces. The driver took a large swig from a whiskey bottle. The other had a big and surprisingly round nose. They had been careful not to address each other by name so I made up my own.

Bozo said, "Let's stop. We need to reconnect the license plate lights on the trailer. We don't want to get stopped."

Boozer grunted and pulled off on an exit in the middle of nowhere. "Watch the scrawny runt. Try not to kill him. He's worth more alive." He got out and returned about five minutes later.

Bozo tied me up with the duct tape while Boozer was gone. "What took so long?"

Boozer chugged some more whiskey, put the truck in gear, and took off with a roar. "Got rid of that tire from the Travel-All. Rolled it far enough from the road so it won't be found."

"Any chance we'll get caught?"

"None." Boozer added, "Those two broads were so shaken up by their spin-out that they won't be able to ID us or the truck. It was dark. Our hats were pulled low over our eyes. This truck was headed for Mexico City. Won't be missed for days. We'll reach our buyer in Tijuana in a few hours. Easiest money we ever made."

Any hopes I had of being rescued were dashed by those words.

"Those poor bastards in Mexico City!" Bozo chuckled. "News said it was a huge quake."

"Who knows? Maybe our buyer will sell this load of medical supplies back to 'em on the black market." Boozer added with a cruel laugh.

"I'm glad you thought of taking the trucker and kid with us."

"Buyer said some folks were desperate for fresh body parts."

"Can't get any fresher than the ones inside that kid, but we could have had fun with one of the broads before selling her." Bozo chortled.

I flinched and suddenly felt very hot as a wave of nausea rolled over me. The taste of bile rose in my throat. *"My God! I've got to get out of here!"* I screamed to myself.

Boozer took another long swig from the whiskey bottle. "The old guy still alive?"

"Yeah. Barely. I checked when I tied up the kid."

"Offering to give me a ride is the last mistake he'll ever make."

"I wish you hadn't hit him so hard," Bozo sighed.

"Whiskey bottle was handy. Besides, I was the one who sat on the piece of broken glass. My ass still hurts."

Bozo complained, "He might die before we get to our buyer in Tijuana."

"We'll be there in a few hours. Maybe his organs will be fresh enough even if he dies."

"Maybe. Either way, we're gonna be rich when we sell the truck, cargo, and body parts!"

My mind raced. Did I hear them say "broken glass?" Maybe some shards fell on the floor back here or in the space between the seats in the front. I let my taped hands fall and brushed my fingers along the floor. Inch by inch, I felt around in the dark.

Several minutes later, I was rewarded by a stabbing pain in my middle finger. I bit my lip to keep from making any noise and picked up a piece of glass about an inch wide and two-and-a-half inches long. One end was rounded and smooth. It must have been part of the mouth of the bottle. The other end was sharp and pointed. A smile broke out as I realized how useful this shard could be.

I laid it next to me and felt around for my jacket pocket. Wrong pocket. Damn! I found my handkerchief in the other pocket and pulled it out. I laid the handkerchief on the glass, folding it over the rounded edge. I held the cloth in my right hand and was about to cut the duct tape on my wrists when Boozer blurted, "I think I see a cop."

Bozo looked out his side mirror, stared for a moment, and said, "Yeah. Highway Patrol."

"I'm not speeding. We should be okay."

They continued to look at their mirrors.

I'd hoped to have time to cut myself free before making my move, but having a cop so close might be my best chance. Maybe my only chance. No time to think. Now or never! I leaned forward and jammed the point of the shard as hard and far as I could into Bozo's neck and yanked it toward me with all my strength, trying to make as big a gash as I could. The shard flew out of my hand as Bozo screamed and tried to grab both his neck and me. I pulled out of reach just in time.

Startled, Boozer almost lost control of the truck, weaving into other lanes as he fought to steady and slow it down.

Bozo fought to stop the blood gushing from his neck with his left hand while trying to undo his seat belt with his right. He got out of his seatbelt, pulled out his handkerchief and jammed it into his wound. Then he turned to face me. I didn't have to see his eyes to know death was in them.

I flung my jacket over the seat onto Boozer's head letting it fall over his face. I pulled the jacket as hard as I could with both hands, using my body weight as I fell back onto the bed. Boozer panicked and let go of the steering wheel as he tried to pull off the impromptu blindfold. The rig swayed wildly.

I tried to kick Bozo away with my bound feet and struggled to keep from losing my grip on the jacket. Bozo got a hand on the toe of one of my shoes. Just as he began to pull me toward him, Boozer panicked and locked up the brakes.

I lost my grip on my jacket when I slammed into the back of the driver's seat, and Bozo lost his grip on me. He fell backwards, headfirst into the windshield. The glass cracked, but held. Stunned, Bozo clambered toward me, a trickle of blood from his head joining the much larger stream from his neck.

The truck crashed into a large gully, and the impact drove Bozo back into and through the shattering windshield. He landed in a heap and didn't move.

Boozer was stunned and, from the sound he made when his torso slammed into the steering wheel, he might have busted some ribs. He threw off my jacket and roared like a wounded carnivore, "I'll break your neck, you little runt!"

When he turned to get me, he noticed the flashing emergency lights from the patrol cruiser. He jumped out of the passenger side of the truck and ran into a darkened field.

It was then I remembered being a little boy and, whenever I saw 18-

wheelers, I'd extend my elbow with my fist in the air and pump it up and down so the truckers would blow their air horns. I reached over the door side of the driver's seat and pulled the air horn cord, making it blow until the patrolman gently pried it from my trembling hands.

Blood Oaths

The man was in his early forties. A trickle of sweat dripped down his forehead, stinging his right eye. He blinked rapidly, his eyes already irritated by too little sleep for too long. White lines rushed past, along with everything else he saw with blurry eyes.

He stomped on the accelerator and the engine bucked and roared in protest but complied, a wheeled horse being raked with vicious spurs. The man looked at the clock on his dashboard for the hundredth time, willing it to move slower. *"I can still reach her in time,"* he thought.

He crested a hill and saw, too late, the jack-knifed big rig blocking the lanes. The trucker desperately tried signaling him to slow down. The man in the car hit the brakes and swerved right. It crashed through a guard rail, plunged down a steep slope, glanced off a large tree, and somersaulted sideways before hitting a jagged boulder with a screeching blow. Atop the incline, a slow-motion chain-reaction landslide followed the path the car had taken.

The man tried to open his eyes, but blood was running into them from a jagged gash in his forehead. He could barely see, even after repeatedly wiping it away with his shirt sleeve. Other than that one arm, he couldn't move. His torso was wedged between a bent steering column and compressed seat. He could tell by the unnatural angles of his legs that they were broken in multiple places. Probably several ribs, too. He smelled gasoline all over everything inside the cage that had been his car.

A moment later a rock that had been dislodged by the rolling car hit a piece of metal at just the right angle to create a spark, igniting the gas. It only took two seconds before the flames reached him. He could do nothing but try to protect his face with his one good arm. His screams echoed throughout the small canyons, reaching the ears of the helpless trucker, who collapsed to his knees in horror.

— —

Lucas Barnett writhed in his bed, bathed in sweat. He jerked awake. He'd had the nightmare again—the same one every night for the last two weeks. It seemed so real that he could feel the heat of the flames and hear the screams. Each time, he never got a good look at the man's face, but somehow, he knew the man was his father.

The young man lay there thinking *"what do I really know about him?"* He could have died many years ago or still be alive. I don't remember him at all. He left when I was a baby. Mom never said anything about him when I begged her to describe him. I don't even have a picture of him or know what he looked like. Heck, I don't know if he was tall or short, fat or thin. For the ten-thousandth time, such questions swirled in his mind, but no answers came. Lucas didn't notice that, for the first time, he asked questions about his father using the past tense.

Now Mom's dead and I'll probably never know about him. Her death had been sudden. The police called it an accident, but he doubted it. His mom was deathly afraid of heights; so afraid that she never ventured out onto the balcony of her tenth-story apartment. Lucas also knew that she hadn't committed suicide. Only two days before her death, she'd told Lucas how excited she was about her long-planned cruise to the Bahamas, only two weeks away, with her dearest friend. Her sudden death had jarred him to the core.

Now, this nightmare stalked him about someone he believed was his father. He decided to find answers to questions that haunted him.

Barnett was his mother's maiden name. No one told him the name of his father, but he saw a name he'd never heard before when he went through his mother's papers. In an unmarked folder that his mom had hidden away, he found a newspaper article about a man named Jacob Makepeace.

Lucas searched for information about people with that name all day and into the evening. He was deep in thought when he heard a soft rapping on his front door. He sighed with annoyance as he looked at the clock. 10:37?! "Who comes to the door so late at night?" he asked himself with a tinge of anger and fear.

As he carefully opened the door, he saw a man quickly back away from the light that streamed out of the entryway, as though the stranger had been scalded. He remained in the shadows as he urgently whispered, "I'm your father's friend. Please help me." The stranger reached out a hand to make a pleading gesture. As it came into the light, Lucas instinctively pulled back. It was covered in blood.

In spite of his concern, Lucas helped the man inside and onto a couch. The man began talking before Lucas had a chance to close the door. "I'm John Fenton. Your dad and I were friends in high school."

"Wait!" Lucas blurted. "You're hurt and should get to a hospital right..."

"NO! They're hoping I'll do that so they can finish the job." He pulled a bloody hand away from a jagged gash that began a few inches above his belt line. He quickly covered it again as blood gushed from the wound.

Lucas grabbed some clean towels and helped Fenton slow the bleeding. "I can't go to the hospital. Justin Slater and his thugs will kill me. They already got your mother."

The news was a hammer-blow to Lucas.

"I'd be dead, too, but saw 'em coming. Was getting in my car when Justin shot me. Lost them in traffic. They won't stop 'til I'm dead."

"What about my father?"

"Died in a car crash on the way to your mom's. He tried to warn her."

Lucas reeled, a balled fist against his lips. Fast, sharp breaths, trying to hold it together.

"We're all in danger. Fenton coughed, his breathing shorter. "Jennifer. You."

"Who's Jennifer?"

"My daughter."

"Daughter?"

Fenton nodded.

"How did all this start?"

"I was always getting into trouble. Your father was a straight arrow. Most loyal man I ever met. Never gave up on me."

Pride welled up in Lucas. He'd waited to hear such words all his life.

Fenton winced as he adjusted the make-shift bandage, then continued, "I started doing drugs. Gambling. He tried to help me. I wouldn't listen." Fenton shook his head sadly. "Got in way over my head. Justin and his thugs came to break my knee caps. Jake came from outta nowhere. Decked Justin and one of his gorillas. They pulled guns."

Lucas inhaled sharply and realized he'd been holding his breath.

Fenton continued, "Neighbor must have called the cops. Uniforms everywhere. Justin's gang started shooting. Killed a cop. Wounded others. Cops nailed some of Justin's goons. He turned his gun on us. Told us to pick up the guns of a couple of his downed men or he'd kill us. We knew he would and grabbed the guns. That's when the cops rushed us."

"Oh..."

"Yeah. Justin threw down his gun. Said we were trying to kill him.

Cops didn't buy it."

The wounded man sighed. "They didn't believe our story, either. Too much cops' blood had been spilled. Someone had to pay."

Lucas exhaled sharply, the news a punch in the gut.

"The three of us rotted in different prisons for nearly twenty years."

Lucas wanted so much to disbelieve it but knew it was true.

"Justin blamed us for everything. Vowed he'd kill us and our families when he got out."

Terror and rage built inside Lucas.

"We were all convicted of the same crimes. Got out at about the same time. Justin's prison was closer to where your mom lived."

Lucas didn't want to hear any more but knew he must.

"Jake called your mom and said he was on his way. He told her to sit tight at a neighbor's. Neither made it."

Lucas silently took the steady blows, each burning away a little more of the young man he'd been. He began to feel old. Very old. "We can hide."

"Too late for that. Can't hide all the blood. They'll finish me off soon. My wife died of cancer, so next they'll come for Jennifer and you.

Lucas almost blurted, "Maybe they won't find her" but knew it wasn't true.

"I headed toward Burton Peak Wilderness Area."

"Why there?"

"Jennifer is camping there with two friends... Somewhere along Barrett Creek."

"I know that area. Spent a lot of time there. Isolated. Rugged."

"Was on my way to warn her. Realized I'd bleed out before I got there. Came here instead."

"We've got to warn her!"

"No! YOU'VE got to warn her. I'll be dead soon... Loss of blood or when Justin finds me."

Lucas knew Fenton was right. He was nearly dead already. It was getting harder for him to talk.

"Find my daughter before they do. Please help her! I don't want her to die. I've been so stupid!" With great effort, Fenton pulled out his wallet and handed a photo to Lucas. It was partially covered in blood from the wounded father's hand. Lucas carefully wiped away the sticky red liquid. He was greeted by friendly emerald-green eyes and a stunning smile, long brown hair, a pert nose, and a few freckles. "Beautiful, isn't she?" Fenton said, more a statement than question.

"She is indeed." Lucas thought for a moment, looked up from the photo. "What if Jennifer doesn't believe me? I'm a stranger to her."

Fenton thought for a moment and then smiled. "When she was a baby, I used to tickle her nose with my eyelashes. She'd giggle. Her mom took a picture of me giving her those 'Butterfly Kisses.' She wrote to me that Jennifer loved that photo. Always keeps it on her nightstand. Tell Jennifer that knowing she did that helped keep me from going crazy all those years I was locked up."

After a moment, Lucas asked, "What does Justin look like?"

"He's 6' 4". Blond hair. Before the shootout with the cops, your father broke Justin's nose. Gave him a gash over his right eye." Fenton beamed. "When I saw Justin this morning, his nose still looked broken. He's now got a jagged scar over his right eye."

Lucas nodded, committing the visual to memory. "How will you protect yourself?"

"I brought a gun. Now, get out of here. Out the back way. Don't drive your car. Run. Call a cab when you get away. Pay cash. Got some?"

"Yes."

"Good! Take all the money you can. Go!"

Lucas didn't know what to say, so he just nodded, grabbed his cash, and ran out the back door. He scrambled over the back fence and made it about 100 feet down the street behind his when the gunshots started. They didn't last long. He knew his father's best friend was dead, and now they'd be coming for him and a girl he'd never met but had to try to warn. A cold chill ran down his spine. He ran as fast as he could while avoiding the glare of the streetlights.

Lucas didn't need a cab. He called a buddy who worked nights only seven blocks away. Thirty minutes later, Lucas roared out of a parking lot headed for the wilderness and an unknown fate.

He knew Justin would find out from Jennifer's neighbors or landlord where she'd gone. But, the Burton Peak Wilderness Area was huge. She could be anywhere. Hopefully, she kept to her plan to stay somewhere near Barrett Creek so he could find her first.

Along the way, he made a mental list of things he might need. He remembered a store on this route that was a cross between a truck stop and sporting goods outfitter. It stayed open all night for truckers and other travelers. He ran in and grabbed each item from the list he'd created in his mind: headlamps, two of the biggest knives he could find, rope, fishing line, and a canteen. On his way out, he stopped at a water fountain and filled the canteen.

Then he remembered that Burton's Peak had a ranger who lived near the entrance of the park. He asked the clerk, "Doesn't a ranger live year-round at Burton Peak?"

"Yeah. George comes in all the time. Gets a lot of his supplies here."

"Happen to have his phone number?"

"Yup." He looked in an old folder of emergency numbers, scratched a number on a scrap of paper, and handed it to Lucas.

"Thanks!" Lucas shouted as he ran out the door. He looked at his watch. 2:07 a.m. He dialed the number as he thought, "Ranger George isn't going to be very happy with me." The phone rang six times. An irritated, raspy voice answered, "Burton Peak."

Lucas explained the situation as fast as he could. At first, the ranger thought it was a prank call, but, as the story unfolded, it was clear it was all too real.

"I saw the three women you're talking about. They said they planned to camp about seven miles up Barrett Creek. That's nearly five miles beyond where the road ends. It's dark, and the trail and terrain are treacherous. Only a fool would be out walking around here tonight. Odds are that Justin fellow and his gang are holed up for the night somewhere. Probably won't arrive until after daybreak."

Lucas sighed with relief. "I guess you're right."

"To be on the safe side, I'll alert the sheriff and have a bunch of deputies waiting for them when they arrive. Don't worry, son, we'll get them."

Lucas allowed himself to feel hopeful for the first time since he answered the knock on his door. Was it only three and a half hours ago? It seemed like forever.

The ranger said, "Someone's knocking on the door. May be an injured camper. Stay on the line. I need more info from you. I'll be right back."

Lucas started to yell a warning, but he heard the bump of the receiver being laid down. Then silence. Thirty seconds. "What's happening?" Lucas screamed to himself. Then he heard two shots. Only two. He knew what had happened before the ranger's body hit the floor.

Lucas hung up and called the sheriff's office as he raced for his car. The dispatcher didn't take the ranting man seriously but said she'd send a patrol car to check on the ranger. She added, "It is a big rural county, and the closest unit probably won't arrive for over an hour."

"That's too late and you better send a bunch of cars unless you want a dead deputy."

"Are you making a threat?"

Lucas hung up. He wanted to run away and hide. But he knew Justin would find him just as he'd found the others. Besides, a woman's life was in danger, perhaps the lives of three women, and he'd promised a dying man that he would try to save her. His mouth was dry. He couldn't even spit. With shaking hands, he grabbed the steering wheel and raced toward Burton Peak.

A quarter mile from the ranger's home, he pulled off a fire trail and parked his car so it couldn't be seen from the main road. He headed into the woods toward the rear of poor Ranger George's cabin.

No lights were on inside. He crept closer. A light flared in one of the back windows. Lucas threw himself against a tree and froze. A moment later the light went out. Someone lighting a cigarette. No doubt one of Justin's men. He looked into the star-filled sky. He noticed with relief that the moon was only a sliver. He thought, *"Good. Dark enough they probably won't see me if I try to get closer."*

He made it to the back wall of the cabin and pressed against it, the big knife in a shaking hand. He listened. Heard the voice of two men talking.

"How long have Justin and the others been gone?" he heard a squeaky-voiced man ask.

"Only five minutes longer than the last time you asked. Quit asking!" came a gruff reply."

"I hope Justin kills her and gets back before dawn. Don't want anyone snooping around." Squeaky voice.

"Should be a snap. They're probably all sleeping. He'll pop all three of 'em with his silencer. Be back in plenty of time. Then we'll get that Make-peace or Barnett kid, or whatever he calls himself, so we can get on with our lives." Gruff voice.

"Not if I can help it," Lucas thought as he headed toward the Barrett Creek trailhead.

It was dark. Too dark. Dangerous. He remembered Ranger George's words, "Only a fool would be out walking around here tonight." Well, he thought, Between Justin and his men, there are a lot of fools on this trail tonight, and I'm the biggest fool of all for trying to catch up to them."

He needed light to see and to move fast. He hoped they weren't waiting to ambush him and were far enough ahead and facing forward so they wouldn't see the red light he used. It was much less visible at night than the white light of most flashlights. Hopefully, he'd see their white light before they'd see his red—IF they weren't waiting to ambush him.

The trail climbed. Steepened. He knew from hiking it many times over the years that it was steep for most of the way and had a lot of hairpin curves. He was still in pretty good shape and hoped that Justin and his city boys weren't. With luck, none of them would be familiar with the trail. Both factors might slow them down and allow him to gain ground. He also knew a couple of short-cuts. They were more treacherous but might help him to get ahead of them.

He found one of the short-cut entry points. Good! It was grown over enough that it was unlikely the others would have noticed. Even if they had, they wouldn't know where it led and, most likely, wouldn't be confident enough to leave the main trail.

When he got to the place where the second short-cut began, he stopped for a moment and listened. He thought he heard something and killed his light. There! Maybe 500 yards down the trail, he saw flickering white lights. Five of them. He'd hoped there would be fewer. Five men to kill three sleeping women. Overkill. At least he was now a little ahead of them.

As he took the short-cut, he thought to himself, "If I'm lucky, I might reach the campsite ten or fifteen minutes ahead of them."

Lucas kept wondering to himself how he'd awaken three sleeping women in the dark in the middle of nowhere without one or more of them screaming. If they screamed, Justin's men would hear it, and that would be the end of them. He came up with several scenarios but each seemed likely to lead to screams.

When the campsite came into view, the answer presented itself in the form of a short and sturdy redhead who had just crawled out of the tent. She probably had to pee. She walked in almost the opposite direction of where he stood. He waited until he heard her stop to do her business, then moved into position to intercept her as she walked back toward her tent.

NOW! He jumped her from behind, covered her mouth with his left hand, and stuck the knife under her chin. She started to struggle and tried to scream, but he let the knife bite slightly into her skin as he frantically whispered into her ear, "Shut up and listen. Five men are coming to kill Jennifer and all of you. They may be about seven minutes away. No time to explain. You've got to trust me or die."

She answered by biting one of the fingers that covered her mouth so hard it bled. Lucas grunted and nearly cried out in pain, but bit his lip instead.

Just then, both noticed a light far down the trail and heading their way. Then another, and another.

The redhead stopped struggling. He moved his hand slightly to allow her to whisper, ready to cover it again if she took a big breath to yell. "OK, maybe you're telling the truth, or maybe those are your friends," she said pointing to the lights creeping ever-closer. "How can I know you're telling the truth?"

"You can't. Jennifer can. Wake up your friends quickly and quietly. Take my knife. I'm trying to save, not kill you! Tell them to bring their coats and shoes. Leave everything else. Hurry!"

The redhead ran to the opening of the tent. He heard urgent whispering. Three terrified women emerged. He went to the only brunette and said, "Jennifer, your dad said to tell you about the Butterfly Kisses he gave you as a baby and the photo your mom took of your dad giving you a Butterfly Kiss that's on your nightstand."

Jennifer nodded in recognition. "Is Dad okay?"

"No time to talk." He pointed at the lights bouncing along the trail. You three head up the trail. Do you know where the trail forks to the left near Barrett Creek about a quarter mile from here?"

"Yeah, at William's Overlook."

"Beneath the overlook is a deer trail. Follow it. When it peter's out, take the next deer trail that veers right. After about a mile it should intersect with the main trail. Don't go to your car or the Ranger's home. He's dead. Two of Justin's men are hiding there in case you slip past Justin or someone calls on the ranger before Justin is off the mountain. Flag down anyone who is alone in a car. Get to the county sheriff. Go now!

"What about you?"

"I know the trail. Will try to slow them down. Give you more time."

She said, "Thanks. Here's your knife. Sue gave it to me."

He said, "Keep it. I have another. Now go."

The women were gone only about two minutes when the first two of Justin's men arrived. They looked exhausted. A minute later Justin showed up, followed by two others that were panting hard. They wasted no time, surrounding the tent. Justin screwed on the silencer to the barrel of his .357. He feared unsilenced gunshots might be heard for many miles and draw unwanted attention. On his signal they all aimed their flashlights through the tents sheer material onto the sleeping bags. Justin quickly shot through the tent emptying his clip into them. The men cheered.

"Shut up!" He hissed. "Something's wrong!" Justin growled. He grabbed a knife and slashed through the side of the tent. He shook the sleeping bags. "Where are they?" he bellowed, his face crimson. He felt the bags again. "They're still warm! They must have just left. Couldn't have gone far."

"Maybe they heard us coming." One of his men guessed.

"Ya think?!" Justin sneered. Well, they are only three unarmed women, and there are five of us with guns."

The men nodded and smiled. Piece of cake.

"They didn't slip past us on the trail." He pointed to a sheer cliff jutting straight up on one side of the trail and a steep drop off on the other. Both could be seen extending at least five hundred yards down the trail they'd just come up, and quite a ways above them. That means their prey had only one way they could go. He turned to point to the trail heading above them when they saw a brief flicker of white light in that direction. "There they are. We've got 'em, boys. Capture 'em alive. Gonna have some fun with 'em. Make 'em wish they'd never been born! Then we'll kill 'em."

Seventy feet up the trail, Lucas saw and heard it all from behind a big tree near the left of the trail. He rushed further up the trail. It became so steep that he was panting before long. He knew the out-of-shape men below him would be even more worn out. He needed them to begin getting spread out with large spaces between them. He had no chance against five armed men bunched closely together, but, if he could spread them out, he just might be able to get one or two and slow down the rest before they got him.

He needed to buy time. He had no illusions as to what would be his fate. The odds against him were simply too high, his options too few and all bad.

The steep slope and darkness were his allies and, with luck, surprise. He found a perfect spot. As the trail continued upward, it was a nearly straight line for about thirty feet and followed a cliff with a steep drop-off on the right side; then the trail veered sharply left. He tied thick fishing line about four inches above the base of a tree immediately across from where the trail formed a sharp "V" next to the trail then let it sag onto the trail, lightly sprinkled dirt over it, and unspooled it in the straight line on the left side of the trail that began just before the "V".

Thirty feet down-trail he wrapped the line around a large tree and hid behind it. He found a big flat rock he could easily handle. Lucas breathed slowly and quietly. He let one man walk past him, then another, then Justin. He didn't like letting men get between him and the women, but it was necessary to have any chance for his plan to work.

The men were spread out, about forty feet apart. A fourth man rushed past him, panting. Lucas grabbed the flat rock. About twenty seconds later, number five hurried abreast of the tree Lucas hid behind. *"NOW!"* Lucas yelled to himself. He hit the man on the back of the head so hard the rock split in two. Lucas heard the sickening crunch as the skull caved in and the man folded like a rag doll. One down. No time to celebrate.

The fourth man heard the noises behind him. He yelled to the men ahead and started racing toward number five. He remembered the sharp curve in the trail and had just begun to slow down as he neared the "V" when Lucas pulled up on the fishing line from his position behind the tree thirty feet down-trail. Number four never saw it coming. He tripped and fell over the cliff. His panicked scream lasted for four seconds and then abruptly stopped, the only evidence of his existence there were faint echoes bouncing off distant canyon walls.

Lucas didn't stop to hear them. He lunged onto the trail desperately trying to locate number five's gun. He knew the others wouldn't fall for his trip line. His hand bumped something metal. He picked it up, felt around for extra clips of ammo and found only one just as a bullet ricocheted off the tree inches from his head. He could see there was not enough cover or concealment for the next two hundred feet down-trail. He needed to make his stand right here. Three against one. Outmanned and outgunned. They also probably had a lot more ammo. This was going to end very badly. Hopefully, he'd buy the women enough time to get away.

Justin and his men began shooting at him from behind trees and boulders.

Lucas tried to conserve ammo, but he couldn't let them flank him or get closer. Then he pulled the trigger and heard a sickening click. Empty! They heard it, too.

Justin yelled, "Rush him. I'll cover you."

Lucas frantically removed the empty clip and put in his only replacement. He reached around the tree and pulled the trigger just in time to drop a man who was only five feet from him. He turned to take a shot at the other man, who had been three steps slower, but his target jumped behind a tree and the bullet meant for him ricocheted away.

Justin saw Lucas' exposed arm and rapidly pulled the trigger three times. A searing pain traveled up Lucas' arm from wrist to elbow with such intensity that Lucas dropped his gun. He desperately tried to pick it up, but his right arm and hand wouldn't work. He grabbed the gun with his left hand firing just in time to wing Justin's only remaining man. The man went down but kept firing. Every time Lucas fired, he knew it might be his last bullet. Then it happened. That sickening click. It was all over now.

Justin stood up with a triumphant smile. Suddenly, he shrieked. His head jerked sharply backwards, accompanied by a terrible crunching noise. Jennifer stood over the collapsing man, holding the blood-stained wedge-shaped rock she'd used to break his neck from behind.

Justin's remaining man turned to shoot Jennifer but saw Sue out of the corner of his eye. She had a rock in her hands and was nearly on him. No time to swing the gun toward her so he threw it down and raised his unwounded arm. Sue nailed him, and the girls tied the crook up and bandaged his arm with a sling. Wendy sat on a boulder nearby and kept his gun aimed at him.

Sue bandaged Lucas' arm. "Just a flesh wound," she said.

"A damn painful flesh wound, if you ask me," Lucas smiled, then winced as the dressing was tightened to help close the wound and slow the loss of blood. "Why did you come back? You could have gotten away!"

Sue shrugged. "Wendy sprained her ankle. Slowed us down. We couldn't leave her. Knew we'd probably be caught anyway."

Jennifer added, "We heard the shooting and knew you needed help. You risked your life to save ours. The least we could do was return the favor."

Legacy

Alone in his car on a bone-chilling, moonless night, he parked on the side of a deserted two-lane road. A nearby bridge towered seventy feet above a roiling river. The young man shivered but not from the cold. He parked close to the span so he wouldn't have far to walk. He chose an unlit bridge to ensure no one would see or interfere.

He struggled to understand how his life had turned so awful so fast. A year ago, he'd been a healthy young man in love with a perfect woman, who had just accepted his marriage proposal. He allowed himself a bitter laugh as nascent tears blurred his vision. "Things aren't so bright now, are they?" he taunted himself, shivering in the cold darkness. His perfect woman proved to be neither perfect nor his, dumping him for another man—but only after they'd told everyone they were engaged.

He closed his eyes, shaking his head; if he shook it hard enough, maybe his nightmare would go away. He wondered how a heart could be so shattered and in so much pain for so long and still keep beating. It should have stopped when she dumped him. That would have saved him from the suffocating weight crushing his chest.

Even sleep betrayed him. Sweet dreams ended in terrible nightmares. Worse, he awakened to find the nightmare was all too real, and he was alone with nothing but the pain of his aching heart.

Touched

"At least you have your health!" he murmured, his voice dripping with sarcasm. Well, he *should* have had his health. Young men *are supposed to be* healthy. He had been for most of his life; long enough to make plans to go to the Naval Academy. That dream died the moment his left lung collapsed. It got so bad that he couldn't walk across a short and level parking lot without stopping halfway and gasping for air.

The pain was hard to take. Being unable to do the things most young men could do was even harder.

He had surgery; then a week in intensive care followed by another week in the hospital and more weeks recuperating at home. His ribs had been split wide enough apart for the surgeon's hands to work inside his chest. Eighteen inches of stitches and nonstop agonizing pain.

At least, he still had one good lung. Until he didn't. His remaining lung began to leak precious air into his chest cavity where it caused even more pain. The lung couldn't properly inflate. He had to go through surgery again, a mere month after the first. He convinced himself he didn't care whether he lived or died during the second surgery. But, that wasn't true. He did care.

He hoped he'd die on the operating table. Even that was denied him. He lived... and suffered mightily all over again.

Both times he was in the hospital, he rarely had visitors, and they never stayed long. His parents came, but they worked long hours to support a big family and had to take care of his younger siblings. His friends... he snorted at that one! With a couple of exceptions, his "friends" had been too busy to visit him during those long lonely agonizing days and nights. Nor did they telephone or send a card or letter.

It was during those gruesome lonely hours that he created his plan.

And, this was it. He shivered again. "It's time."

A movement in the darkness in front of his car interrupted him. He squinted, trying to pierce the blackness. There! Yes, something was moving in his direction. "It's... a... man...."

For a moment, he froze with fear. Why would a man come toward him in the middle of the night in complete darkness on a lonely stretch of road in the middle of nowhere?

He caught himself and silently laughed at his fear. *"Considering what I'm about to do, what do I have to be afraid of?"* he thought to himself. *"If the man kills me, he'll be doing me a favor. Maybe he's going to rob me. Good luck with that, buddy! I've got nothing worth having."*

As the stranger moved closer, the young man could see he was bent over and old. The man staggered and fell. He slowly picked himself up and stumbled forward again. When he was quite near the young man's car, it became clear that he was half-carrying, half-dragging, a huge old suitcase. The stranger fell again and didn't get up.

The young man turned on his headlights and rushed to him. He pulled the prone stranger a couple of feet so he'd be lit by a headlight beam. The fallen man's clothes were worn and thin, far too thin for the punishing winter cold. He appeared very ill as he lay gasping and shivering. His eyes didn't seem to focus properly. He had white, thinning hair that hadn't been cut or combed in quite a while.

The stranger tried to speak but no words came. He tried again, seemingly with every bit of energy he had, but only a faint raspy whisper leaked out between gasps. "Car... broke down... " He took a moment to catch his breath and gather his strength. "Waited... waited too long..." Tears ran down the old man's face from the saddest eyes the young man had ever seen. "I... I've been... a fool..." His voice trailed off and his eyes began to glaze over.

"Hold on! I'll get you to a hospital!" the young man promised, as he prepared to lift him.

Touched

"No time.... No...! Too late... for me." He sobbed, gasping for air.

His mind and eyes appeared to fade, but a violent shiver jarred him back. He blinked repeatedly, as if he were desperately trying to remember something important he needed to say. "GO! Take... suitcase..." The outburst appeared to use the little energy that he had left. More gasping, but weaker. His lips moved, but a strengthening wind drowned his words. The young man leaned closer, so close he could feel the man's breath on his cold ear.

"I wanted... to leave... a legacy," he wheezed with his last breath. The young man sadly watched the final flicker of light leave the tortured man's eyes.

The young man sat in shock. Realizing he still held the dead stranger, he gently laid the old man's head on the ground. Panic swelled. "What do I do? What do I do?"

His fear, adrenaline, and the pleading words of the old man jolted him into action. He grabbed the old heavy suitcase, threw it into his car, jumped in after it, and sped toward home, forgetting all about the bridge and the reason he'd come.

His mind raced. A million questions pounded his brain. Had the stranger been running to something or someone or away from them? Had the old man been in danger? Am *I* in danger? He pounded the steering wheel in frustration, then considered throwing away the suitcase and trying to forget the whole thing, but knew he wouldn't. Couldn't. He needed to know what was inside it that had made the old man so desperate. Hopefully, he'd find answers there. He wouldn't rest until he saw its contents.

He carried the suitcase inside his dark, cold, empty apartment. He'd shut off the heater, figuring he wouldn't need it again. Now he cursed himself for that decision as he fumbled in the darkness for the light switch and then cranked up the thermostat with cold-numbed fingers.

He hauled the suitcase to his worn-out dining room table, pushing clutter out of the way. "What if it's locked?" He mumbled to himself. It wasn't. The latches sprang open so loudly he jumped. He pulled the lid open. His mouth dropped. The battered suitcase was stuffed to the brim with neatly stacked large bundles of $100 bills.

"This has got to be counterfeit!" he blurted to the empty room. A closer look showed that many of the bills had been in circulation. Could it be drug money? His fear soared again. Did the stranger steal it? More questions with no answers.

He scratched his head. That's when he saw two small books wedged into a corner of the suitcase. He carefully pulled them out. The first held a list of names, addresses, and some writing under each listing. Puzzled, he set it aside and opened what he guessed was a journal. The name of the owner was not written inside.

As he turned a page to begin to read, he noticed a small photo inserted between the pages. The old black and white photo showed a handsome and proud young man with his arm around his beautiful bride on their wedding day. He turned it over. Nothing was written on the back. He brought the photo over to a brighter light and looked at it closely. Could the confident, handsome young man in the photo be the same person as the desperate wreck of a human being who had just died in his arms?

He shook off the idea as ludicrous. Then he looked again. Very closely. The same nose. Same chin. Even the shape of the bushy eyebrows. The more he looked, the more certain he was that it was the same man. But who was he? What was his name? Why did he have all this money? He eagerly began reading.

The journal told of an ambitious young man who had married his high school sweetheart, a beauty named Miriam. He climbed the corporate ladder as fast as he could, working long, hard hours. They bought a new house; later, a bigger house and nicer cars. They decided not to have children. Kids would have been expensive and annoying distractions. Their desire for more of everything grew. They had vacation homes, trips around the world, and all the trappings of wealth. They hadn't realized that the word "trap" is in the word "trappings" for a reason.

They decided he could make money faster if he started a business. Long hours became longer still. At some point, Miriam wanted to get off the treadmill. At first she hinted, and then begged him to slow down and to spend more time with her. He was so blinded by his lust for wealth that he couldn't see he was killing their relationship. He kept promising to spend more time with her "next year."

She heard "next year" for five years. She threatened to leave him. He didn't believe her until, one day, she left and never returned.

He went into a tailspin, trying everything to dull the pain. Nothing worked. He ultimately lost all he had. Even his soul.

Then, one night, he had an incredibly vivid dream in which he was, once again, wealthy. Instead of wasting all his money, he found people who had done wonderful things for the world and who badly needed money. He gave it to them.

He woke up feeling happier than he'd felt in decades. He had a reason to live again. He set aside everything that numbed his pain and began to build his fortune all over again. He worked harder than ever and saved as much as possible. He invested it wisely and watched it grow as the years ticked by.

He was so focused on his goal, he didn't notice his hard work and frugality turned into something else. Something darker. His addictive personality led him to a different extreme. He became a miser.

Once again, he forgot to stop and enjoy life, becoming so obsessed with rebuilding a fortune that even old Scrooge would have been impressed—at least until Ebenezer's awakening that fateful Christmas.

Nothing else mattered to the old man but to build great wealth so he could give it away to those who had done great, selfless things for the world. He collected a list of people who had done such things and were badly in need of cash. He put their names, addresses, and what they had done in the second journal, so when he'd earned enough money, he'd give it to them. It was his way of atoning for wasting his life. But, alas! As with Miriam, the amount he had was never "enough."

He felt ill but didn't want to "waste" money going to a doctor. He was able to deal with the illness on his own for quite a while. He lost weight, a lot of it. Then one day, after he was barely able to get out of bed for two weeks, he dragged himself to the doctor.

Cancer—the last stage of a fast-moving virulent form of it. He had perhaps days to live. He panicked! "NO! This can't be happening. I'm finally ready to do some good for the world and now I'm dying!?!"

The last entry in the journal was written with a shaky hand and was smeared with what appeared to be tear-stains:

"I've been such a fool to wait so long! It's time. I've got to get this money to those people before death catches up to me. I want, I NEED, to leave this legacy."

The last words the old man had spoken came back to the young man:

"I wanted... to leave... a legacy."

The young man knew what must have happened next. The dying old fool had stuffed the suitcase full of cash and was driving to a small town where the first potential recipient of his cash lived when his car broke down at night on a lonely two-lane road in the middle of nowhere. He'd gotten out of the car in freezing cold weather and tried to take the suitcase on foot.

"What a crazy, stupid, old fool!" The young man thought. The old man wasted his entire life. “Well, thank you for all this money! I finally can do all the things I’ve dreamed of doing! I’m rich!” He fell asleep dreaming of the things he would buy with it.

The next morning, he learned on the news the man’s name was Harold Nashton. The story went on to say the police thought Mr. Nashton died of what appeared to be exposure. No foul play was suspected, but an autopsy was being done.

“So, your name was Harold Ashton. Thank you for making me a very rich young man!”

— —

The now-rich young man couldn’t quite believe his good fortune. He stared at the most beautiful car he’d ever seen. It was perfect! The exact make, model, and color he’d lusted after for years. All he had to do was sign the paperwork, pay the money, and it would be HIS!

He reached for a pen. He noticed his hand was shaking. “Must be all the excitement!” He thought to himself. He found the signature line, lowered the pen to the page, and... froze. *“What the...? Sign the form!”* He screamed to himself. *“What are you waiting for?!”* His mind raced. *“Maybe I should check out other makes and models first just to be sure I get the best fit for me. Yeah, that sounds like the right thing to me. I’ve waited this long, I can wait until tomorrow. Just to be sure.”*

He quickly explained the situation to the seller and left. But he didn’t look at other cars. He looked at Harold Nashton’s little book with the list of names, addresses, and descriptions instead.

— —

A young flight attendant who was tragically burned while saving the lives of passengers in a downed commuter plane answered a knock on the door to find no one there. Before she closed the door, she noticed a gift bag with colorful tissue paper and an envelope on top. She smiled, looked around, and said, "This is nice of someone."

When she grabbed the bag, she needed both hands to lift it, partly because of the weight of the bag and partly because of the damage to her hands. She dragged, then hauled it up to a sturdy table and pulled the tissue paper away. *"There MUST be some mistake!"* she thought when she saw the bag was full of hundred dollar bills. Hundreds of them. Maybe thousands! *"Who...? Why...?"*

She remembered the envelope with her name on it. With shaking hands, she tore it open and pulled out a greeting card. Joyous tears fell. Her blurry eyes made it hard to see the words. She wiped tears away with the backs of her hands and read:

"Thank you for making the world a better place.

With Love,

Harold Nashton"

— —

The young man smiled as he walked away. "You know, I could get used to this," he said as he opened the little book to look up the next name on the list.

Nightmare

Well before Royce Maclean came out of the fog of anesthesia from his brain surgery in the CIA-secured operating room, he urgently whispered, "Did you get them? Was it in time?"

— —

His mission started well. It was as straightforward as it was critical and difficult: Infiltrate the super-secret Black Snake organization that seemed to pop up out of nowhere and threatened the world. Other agents discovered parts of the puzzle, but what they discovered was terrifying. Even the limited information they reported cost three agents their lives.

The Black Snake plan was pure genius. The world could respond to two, perhaps three, limited outbreaks of highly virulent different diseases, but what if ten or twelve new diseases were unleashed at over two hundred strategic points around the globe? What if the only people who had the cure were the leaders of Black Snake?

Black Snake developed at least a dozen new strains of bio weapons for which they created vaccines and antidotes for themselves. They were producing the toxins fast and would soon have enough to distribute them to their 200 target sites. Their calculations indicated that over 98% of humanity would be wiped out within a week.

Black Snake even created two versions of the vaccine they called

Master-Key. "Master-Key A" vaccinated people against all of the new strains simultaneously. It required a single dose and was only given to the leaders and most trusted members of Black Snake. For everyone else who was willing to pay all they had to keep themselves and/or their loved ones alive, Black Snake created a watered-down version, "Master-Key B," that required frequent booster shots of the vaccine. Anyone who wanted to live would remain at the mercy of Black Snake for the rest of their enslaved lives. The richest could pay the most; they would have the option of buying continued life every three weeks—the maximum length of time each booster shot worked.

That strategy would minimize rebellion of the relatively few survivors. What good was taking over the world if the world was in constant rebellion?

Members of Black Snake were not doing it for political, ideological, or religious reasons. It was greed that drove them... not simple greed... absolute greed. Black Snake would soon own everything and everyone. Anyone who lived long enough to cross them would die in horrifying ways.

It wasn't a coincidence that both versions of the vaccine not only looked identical to each other, but to what Black Snake referred to as "The Killer Cocktail." That was the combination of the dozen deadly new superstrains they'd created. One wouldn't know when being injected with either version of the vaccine whether they were actually receiving the identical-looking lethal cocktail and were about to die an agonizing death.

The world threw their best assets at the Black Snake. Many agents attempted to infiltrate the organization. Eighteen had made some progress. Three made it far enough to transmit the parts of the plot that were known. Of the eighteen, seventeen agents had died from the "Killer Cocktail."Only one hope remained alive: Royce MacLean. And he'd been shot in the head.

He discovered where they manufactured the "Master-Key A" and stole a vial so it could be analyzed and, if possible, quickly mass produced. He even managed to steal a device that contained the names of the couriers who were to deliver the killer cocktail, the method of delivery, and the locations that were the initial targets. But, before he could escape with the critical items, the theft of the vial was discovered.

Royce MacLean tried to make a run for it through a maze of buildings with Black Snake operatives in hot pursuit. Several times, they surrounded him, but, each time, he found a way to elude them. Sometimes he ambushed and took down his pursuers while they waited to ambush him, and sometimes he used more subtle tricks of the trade. It was Cat-and-Mouse, but the cat learned quickly that this mouse could bite. That slowed them down a bit.

He shook some of them off by breaking a restroom mirror, carrying it to a window and reflecting a ray of light from a small spotlight into another building. He pulled the mirror away after they saw the flash.

"See that?"

"Yeah. Better call it in. Looks like the bastard may have gotten past us again."

MacLean waited until they re-directed the search and before moving again.

He'd been unable to smuggle in a communications device. Agents had gotten caught and killed trying to do so. Black Snake also jammed all com signals in their facilities, so a few different extraction locations and times had been established before the mission. Each time he got close to an extraction area, it was overrun by Black Snake operatives, and the extraction teams were slaughtered.

The chase lasted ten-and-a-half grueling hours. He was on foot and running from building to building at night in an industrial complex comprising hundreds of buildings housing multiple hundreds of companies. Most of the buildings were dark, many were interconnected, and each was configured differently. It was truly a maze he ran through as he fought to escape his pursuers.

The last extraction team was getting desperate. They abandoned the designated rendezvous point and tracked some of the pursuers who were running on the outside of the buildings trying to surround MacLean.

MacLean ran into the darkened reception area of a company. The front door was blocked by the Black Snake operatives. The noose closed in on him again. With a power burst, Agent Westfield drove into the armed men blocking Royce's way and crashed through the glass front doors in a hail of bullets. An agent in the passenger seat and one in the backseat let loose with fully automatic weapons hanging out windows on both sides of the car, laying down suppression fire. Royce ducked and ran to the car as a passenger door was flung open for him. He leaned in just as a bullet hit him in the head. The agent in the rear seat grabbed and pulled him inside, yelling, "GO! GO! GO!" Westfield slammed the car in reverse and backed away from the withering fire. Black Snake men chased after them firing as they went. Additional agents and law enforcement units arrived on the scene and blocked pursuers. The agent who pulled Royce into the car heard him blurt, "Almost captured. Hid vial and info. L-..." before Royce lost consciousness. The agent attempted to slow the bleeding.

They brought him to the medical team standing by to begin analyzing the antidote. Royce survived but was so near death, the chief surgeon decided the best way to keep him alive was to induce a coma to stabilize him.

The brain specialists were advised their patient held the key to the future of humanity in his brain. They thought they could operate and save his life, and perhaps all or nearly all of his faculties, but the surgery might also kill him, and if the first one didn't, follow-up surgeries might. They decided to try an experimental option and lifted the coma to get him to experience more of a heavy dream-like state, then tried to coax his brain to show them where he'd hidden the vaccine and critical information. They saw him steal the items and begin his getaway into the maze of darkened buildings. He began to relive the chase, but with the new experimental procedure the scientists could "see" what his brain "saw" each step of the way. It was like a watching a very blurry video that began to play from the point when the chase began. It was slow, frustrating work. Hopefully, once Royce's relived nightmare led them to the moment he hid the items, they could see where the stuff was hidden and send teams to retrieve them.

The crew was dismayed at how many twists and turns he made. It was harder and harder to track his movements through the darkened corridors. Between the uniqueness of the layout of each building, the darkness, and the number of times he needed to backtrack or go in circles to elude his pursuers, they often lost track of where he was. Even if Royce's nightmare showed where he hid the items, it was likely they still wouldn't know where "there" was. They increased the number of people monitoring and analyzing every aspect of his dream.

As the dream continued, Royce's heart and respiration rates climbed to dangerous levels. He often had to fight two or three men at a time. The scientists were amazed at how quick and deadly MacLean was. They had to keep being reminded to watch *where* he was, not what he was doing.

His enemy was also learning fast. When he took out one or two men, the next groups he encountered had three or four. When he took those out, the number of men in each pursuit group tripled.

But MacLean also used the darkness and maze to his advantage. Even when some pursuers new where he was, trying to communicate the location to others was very difficult. The others often had to navigate through their own mazes to try to get to him, and often by the time they got to where he'd been he was long gone.

MacLean avoided using the weapons he'd taken off the pursuers as much as possible. They didn't have silencers and shooting them would have helped Black Snake know exactly where he was through triangulation of the noise.

The CIA sent agents disguised as various repair and installation vendors into several of the buildings. They'd be in place if MacLean's dream showed the scientists where the items were hidden. The teams tried to find the objects on their own, but the complex was so vast that the search could take years.

It was a risky balancing act. If the teams moved any more aggressively, Black Snake operatives would learn Royce hid them in the complex instead of bringing them to the extraction vehicle. Black Snake would then burn the entire complex to the ground. As it was, the organization would surely attempt to move up the target date for unleashing hell on earth. The race was on; it was Winner-Take-All; and Black Snake had a huge, perhaps insurmountable, head start.

For Royce, it was a never-ending nightmare. From building to building, office to office, dark void to brief bright light, then plunging back into darkness again; a hellish nightmare where every turn could lead to a dead end, ambush, or a hail of bullets. He panted, unable to catch his breath; sweat ran into his eyes, stinging them and making it even harder to see. His shirt was drenched in sweat. He tripped in the darkness several times and smashed headlong into whatever was in front of him. Each time he fell, he protected the vial and its precious contents. He became so exhausted that all he wanted to do was lie down and sleep, but still he ran. Sheer will and spite drove him to keep going.

Another cluster of buildings. Another maze. "Where am I? When will this nightmare end?"

— —

Bright light. Royce was lying on his back coming out of the fog of anesthesia. "Did you get them? Was it in time?"

He looked in the eyes of Agent Christine Westfield. "Yes, Royce. We did. YOU did it!" She squeezed his hand. He gave a weak smile and tried to squeeze her hand back but faded into the fog.

Days later, Royce's recovery was still on track and his strength and faculties began to return. Each time he opened his eyes, he saw the smiling but worried face of Christine. This surprised him that she seemed to care like that. He was usually very good at reading people, but she hid her feelings from him. Until now. He was disappointed at himself for not noticing signs earlier but happy at the revelation.

Royce said, "I was surrounded; about to be captured for the fourth or fifth time. I thought for sure they had me so I hid the items in the hope you all could find them. But I eluded them again, and the chase lasted much longer than I thought it would."

Christine replied, "You were a genius to hide them on top of a lit company name sign. We'd lost where you were but, by putting it on that Liatronix sign, we knew instantly where to find them. Well done!"

Christine provided a longer situation report now that he was feeling stronger. "We got the information in time. Intelligence and law enforcement agencies from around the world are capturing the Black Snake operatives. It was relatively easy in most cases. The info you obtained told us who they were and the exact location where they planned to unleash the diseases. Just in case we miss any, huge batches of "Master-Key A" are being produced and staged at strategic locations around the world for rapid deployment to wherever it might be needed. Gradually, everyone will be inoculated with it.

"We're trying to take the couriers alive and are interrogating the survivors. So far, little useful info is coming from them because they were so far down the chain of command—little more than mules actually—but you never know and we've gotta try."

"Enough business! How 'bout joining me for a cocktail when I get outta here?"

"I'd love to, Royce." She smiled and squeezed his hand.

About the Author

Russ lives with his wife in Campbell, California. They've been married since 1979 and have three children and three grandsons. In addition to enjoying his family and friends, and his dual passions for investing and writing, Russ loves to spend time in nature, especially near rivers and streams that run through giant redwood groves, and near beautiful beaches. He enjoys watching classic movies, reading, and tending to his small fern garden and redwood grove. Russ manages the investments of the wealth management firm he founded in 2003. He has published fourteen books.

Russ Towne's books can be found on Amazon.com.

Russ's Amazon Author Page can be found at www.amazon.com/author/russtowne.

Russ Towne's titles include:

Fiction

Palpable Imaginings: An anthology of fictional short stories by several writers in various genres.

Nonfiction

From the Heart of a Grateful Man: A collection of heart-warming and often humorous stories about romance, relationships, and family.

Reflections of a Grateful Man: An anthology of heart-warming, uplifting, and often humorous stories about life.

Slices of Life: Selected writers share inspiring, humorous, and heart-warming stories about many facets of life.

Poetry

Heart Whispers: A powerful and touching anthology of the selected works of over twenty poets.

Books for Young Children

V. G. and Dexter Dufflebee

The Grumpadinkles

Ki-Gra's REALLY, REALLY BIG Day!

The Duck Who Flew Upside Down

Clyde and Friends

Clyde and Hoozy Whatzadingle

Clyde and I Help a Hippo to Fly

Rusty Bear and Thomas Too

Clyde and I

Zach and the Toad Who Rode a Bull

Children's App Based on Characters from His Clyde Books:
Clyde and Friends children's app developed by e-book-design.com using characters from Russ's series of Clyde books.
www.ClydeandFriends.com

Russ's Blogs:

A Grateful Man (Nonfiction uplifting posts): RussTowne.com

A Grateful Man's Poetry: AGratefulMansPoetry.com

Imaginings of a Grateful Man (Fictional short stories):
ImaginingsofaGratefulMan.com

Clyde and Friends (on writing children's stories):
CydeandFriends.com

www.ingramcontent.com/pod-product-compliance
Lightning Source LLC
Chambersburg PA
CBHW060623310726
48982CB00003B/656

* 9 7 8 0 6 9 2 7 0 0 0 8 2 *